Goose River Anthology, 2021

Edited by

Deborah J. Benner

Goose River Press
Waldoboro, Maine

Library of Congress Card Number: 2021944604

ISBN: 978-1-59713-235-0 paperback
ISBN: 978-1-59713-236-7 hard cover

First Printing, 2021

Cover photo by Kristy Benner.

Published by
Goose River Press
3400 Friendship Road
Waldoboro, ME 04572
email: gooseriverpress@gmail.com
www.gooseriverpress.com

Authors Included

Authors Included

Authors Included

Dedicated to our teachers.

Special thanks to Sue Campagna for her wonderful help in proofing the book.

Sandra Conlon
Steamboat Springs, CO

The Father

"Who is she, Addie?" Although the question sounded irrelevant to him when he asked it, a dimly lit answer seemed to be pushing itself out of the darkness, beyond reach, so he heard himself repeat the question three more times in succession. He saw a small child with hair the color of sunlight running toward him, as he waited on the porch of a house he hadn't lived in for years. "Is that you, Ellie?" he asked in the same puzzled manner. He was speaking to the small child.

"Yes, Pop. It's me." She spoke kindly to him, but he heard only the "Pop" part and couldn't make sense of the other words, which sounded to him like static interrupting a radio program. There she was on a Sunday afternoon, lying on the floor with the funny papers, her hair in pigtails now, and her brothers playing Monopoly at the dining room table. They were arguing over Park Place.

"I've come for J.D.'s wedding on Saturday." The sound drifted toward him, fragmented, in slow motion, and disappeared in the air.

"Who's getting married? Are we going somewhere?" He couldn't stop the questions, and this time when she opened her mouth to speak, he thought she was trying to trick him. What she said made no sense, and he heard himself repeat the questions he had already asked. He held up his hand, but she was still talking. Now he perceived the kindness in her voice but not the sense or meaning in her words, and he saw her dressed in black, accepting an award of some kind while he and his wife applauded. They had travelled some distance to see her because she had been away for a long time. He heard his words tumble from his mouth again. "Where ya' been?"

"I live in Altoona now, with Frank. I'll be here a week...after the wedding, I'll...." Weak. Yes, he was feeling

Sandra Conlon
Steamboat Springs, CO

very weak, and her words were like waves rolling onto the shores of his mind, washing away sense and meaning.

"Catch my handkerchief. It's flying away. Catch it." His voice was heavy and lethargic.

"Here ya' go, Pop," she said, as she handed him a fresh, white hanky. He grabbed it with his left hand, dabbed at his right eye, and rolled the cloth into a ball.

"Can't move it," he said, pointing to his right hand. "Won't work. Not connected."

"I know, Dad. It's from the stroke." The sounds washed over him and his heart was filled with great joy, as the two of them started down the aisle. She was beautiful, her skin as pure and lovely as a china doll's. He had been to China once, during the war. No. Japan. It was Japan, before Pearl Harbor, and he had sent her a doll and a pearl ring, but as he looked up from his handkerchief, he didn't know who she was.

"You have a husband?" He heard another question fall out of his mind. "What's he doing there?" And another.

The person standing before him smiled and moved her lips. Water again washed upon the shore, and the sound he heard was like the echo in an old conch shell. Why was her hair so grey? Why did she look familiar? He would wait and ask again later. When his wife came home, she would know.

***

Sylvia Little-Sweat
Wingate, NC

Clematis

The clematis vine
climbs the trellis to unfurl
a royal banner.

Kate Kearns
Scarborough, ME

A Box of Fire Warms Our Home

So hot down by the woodstove
we lost our pants. So hot
my coffee hasn't cooled.
A snow-covered window
lets in white light high up
at the ceiling. Shirts gone, too,
so hot down here we're
in our underwear, our skin
like peanut butter, and puzzle
pieces fudgy in our fingers.
The cats went up ages ago
to windowsills. So hot
our hearts are too fast. So hot
the dust sizzles, like brush fire,
a restorative. The dog pants so hard
he hardly breathes. He won't,
would never, leave us down
here without him to dissolve.

***

Cordula Mathias
Trevett, ME

Suddenly Silver

Salt and pepper
The mirror whispered for years.

Now
Suddenly
Silver.

Irene Zimmerman
Greenfield, WI

Harvesting

When I showed up barefoot between corn rows,
carrying a syrup pail packed with apples from
the orchard, jelly biscuits warm from the oven,
and a thermos of fresh lemonade, Papa wiped
his sweaty face with his red handkerchief
and walked to the front of the wagon. Flory
and Fanny whinnied in reply to whatever it was
he told them and promptly closed their eyes.

We sat on the ground in the mottled shade
of corn stalks. Papa filled two tin cups
of lemonade, handed me one of them, and set
his down between us. Next, he pulled out
his pocket knife, peeled an apple, cut it into
quarters, and gave me two. I watched him wipe
the blade on his overalls and return the knife
to his pocket. I was eleven. I knew about germs.

But Mama always said eating a little dirt wouldn't
kill you. So I chewed my apple and drank lemonade
as Papa began his story of how, the September
he turned seven, he husked corn alongside Grandpa
in this very field. I'd often heard the story, but knew
he loved to tell it. Above us dry sheaves rustled
as I sat contentedly, listening to his face and eyes.

Janet Dorman
Falmouth, ME

Bald Rock Mountain–July 2011

On a Sunday in July, we climbed to the top of Bald Rock Mountain in the Camden Hills in Maine to spread my sister-in-law's ashes. Bald Rock was one of several spots in those hills where Anne liked to hike, and she did so nearly every summer except the last one when the cancer made it physically impossible. I pictured Anne's ashes floating out over the cliff, down the side, over the tops of the trees and maybe even up and out over Penobscot Bay. Perhaps a bald eagle would appear below the cliff, soaring over the treetops as they sometimes did, and some of her ashes would land on its wings. The thought made me smile. Fanciful, I admit, but fun to imagine.

We were a group of six accompanied by Anne's rescue Corgi, Benny. John carried his wife's ashes in a wooden urn stowed in his pack. Their two kids, Tom and Katie, were there, as were her sister, Debby, and her brother, Tom, my husband. Starting off, Benny ran circles around us, herding us in a pack, our shepherd for the climb.

At one time or another, we had all done this hike with Anne, and it seemed familiar to be walking together, talking, catching up, telling stories like we always did. Anyone observing us would see just another group out for a hike in the hills. None of us talked about our particular purpose. There were no plans of what we would do or say. I suppose I had a vague notion that we would stand on the bald rock pate of the cliff and empty the ashes over. In my role as a pastor and chaplain, I was familiar with "cremains," as the ashes are euphemistically called by funeral directors. Some parts are heavy and go easily to the ground. Most are light and will catch the breeze and float.

The last leg of the trail was a bit steep and our group had spread out, so when Tom and I brought up the rear, we spent some time finding the rest of the party. There were lots of people spread out on the rocks and the various ledges, resting, eating and generally taking in the spectacular view of the bay and the islands. We found our party sitting off to the right, out of the sun, beginning a picnic. John was not with them and someone said he was off on the other side of the summit. I went to find him, suspecting that he was looking for a good spot for our purpose. My brother-in-law is an experienced pilot and hang glider; he knows wind currents. When we met up, he looked worried, his whole face furrowed with concern. He took me over to the cliff edge and pointed out that the wind was blowing up from the ocean and that the ashes would blow along the wind's path, back over the mountain and over...*all the other people.*

All the other people, indeed. And their dogs and small children. Somehow in my differing scenarios, I didn't account for *all the other people* being there. Why, I cannot say. Perhaps it was because we took our hikes during the week, so that even in summer, it was not very crowded. But on a beautiful Sunday in July, the top of the mountain was the picnic and rest stop for the masses. Apparently, that fact didn't enter anyone else's scenario either and thus, John's worried look.

"I'm not taking them back," he said, "I'm going to spread them."

I could feel myself being pulled into finding a solution—the professional clergywoman taking over. After all, I had done a lot of the coordinating for Anne's memorial service in February and officiated on the day. Debby had half-jokingly referred to me as the "family chaplain." Shouldn't I fix this? No, I was simply the sister-in-law at this moment. To be other would be officious and this was John's moment. He was doing this for his wife and for his kids. He would figure out what needed to be done.

We rejoined the others and ate our sandwiches, shared some fruit and trail mix, talked about the view and acted and

Janet Dorman
Falmouth, ME

sounded pretty much like everyone else up there. We watched to see if the crowd would thin out, but no one was moving. By this time, I think everyone in our group realized that even if the wind shifted and blew out over the cliff and toward the sea, it would be awkward, to say the least, for us all to get up and start handing around the urn, taking our turns flinging Anne's ashes into the air.

I don't usually think of the top of a mountain as a public place. I take in the view, watch the trees wave in the breeze and the birds soar. I try to identify wildflowers and wonder about the geology under my feet. I benignly ignore the people around me and I expect they do the same with me. I am not actively seeking privacy, but rather hoping to find it in my interior thoughts and ruminations sitting in the company of strangers.

Spreading ashes is a private and intimate act, and I don't think I realized the truth of that until we got to the top of Bald Rock Mountain with all our fellow day hikers. The top of a mountain can be a very public place when you wish to do something that begs for privacy.

John did figure out what to do. Further to the right where we sat for lunch was a small leafy glade with a sward of soft grass surrounded by a stand of small hardwood and evergreen trees. The sun filtered down through the branches. It was quiet and peaceful.

"This will be fine," he declared. "She'll be protected from the sun and in the fall when the leaves are gone, she'll have a view." He removed the top from the urn and began to shake it vigorously over the grass in the glade. Plumes of ash lifted and settled, kept in by the overhanging branches. I thought he must have emptied the urn with the amount that shook out, but he handed it off to the rest of us standing there.

"There's a lot of her left," he observed and handed the urn over so others might take a turn. I stood and bore witness to the family members performing this last ritual. As the

Janet Dorman
Falmouth, ME

ashes emptied out, we stood in silence watching Anne's final dance, when suddenly the air was filled with the song of a hermit thrush. Very secretive birds, they live in the interior of the woods, foraging on the forest floor. Rising up through the trees their song is flute-like and clear, and I cannot hear it without feeling my heart rise in response—a haunting accompaniment to our bittersweet rite.

As the bird sang, each member of the family took a turn spreading some of the ashes that seemed to rise and fall with the notes of the thrush. There were hugs and tears but no words in this moment that was oddly sad and joyful at once. When we finished, we were standing in a line, arms wrapped around each other, facing the glade, watching the last ashes settle, Benny sitting at John's feet.

As if on a director's cue, a butterfly—a White Admiral—flew among the branches. A sign of resurrection, almost too perfect, but hopeful, nonetheless. We stood, arms entwined, absorbing the moment, not wanting to move. It could have ended there on that poignant and lovely note, but it was not to be.

A chipper female voice called out behind us, "Well, if that isn't a family photo op!" Clearly the woman was offering to take our picture, but what could we say? We said nothing, but turned and looked at her, tongue tied and red eyed. She was sensitive enough to realize that this wasn't a family photo op, God bless her for that. She didn't ask any questions, but faded tactfully away, perhaps embarrassed, or at least confused, as to what she may have intruded upon. Not what you would expect on top of a mountain on a sunny Sunday in July.

We gathered up our things and did have one family photo out on the rock, overlooking the bay. Not so different from all the others, after all, but one in our group observed that some of our fellow hikers did go back to the glade, perhaps curious as to what we were up to back there. Maybe our erstwhile family photographer carried a message of strange

Janet Dorman
Falmouth, ME

doings away from prying eyes.

We hiked back down much as we had hiked up—companionable and recalling other Maine adventures with the family, "Do you remember when...?" Benny resumed his shepherding as we headed down the trail. We didn't talk about what we had done, but I know that I was a bit different from when I went up, carrying now a small sense of closure. This had been a date on my calendar since February; an event anticipated and now passed. It only takes the passage of a small but significant moment to wrest something around in one's soul and to open the heart to a new direction.

***

Peggy Trojan
Eau Claire, WI

Small Talk

The crow and the squirrel
Who claim the large tree
outside my balcony,
meet each morning
to pontificate.
Sometimes, I join them.

This morning,
speaking three different languages,
we agreed the weather
has been lousy lately,
and we sure as heck don't need
any more rain.

Published in *Bramble, 2020*

Marcia Annenberg
ME & NY

Crystallization

You inscribe my being
with a path
a route that I can follow
like a map:
You chart my territories
make visible the heights and depths
connecting rivers and by-ways,
so that the whole
becomes traversable
inhabitable:
where before
weeds choked
walls dividing homesteads.

You make my boundaries expand
And yet contract
You draw my myriad selves—
so distinct and diverse
into a whole,
that even I in viewing from afar
can look at and beyond acceptance
or understanding,
enjoy the sap that flows
from the maple I am
whether winter or summer
environs
shake at the core
of my bark.

Karyn Lie-Nielsen
Waldoboro, ME

Nate and The Bluefish

after Olive Pierce photograph

By this time his legs are dock pilings
taking on every wave and roll without fault.
You didn't see him catch a step when the skiff was full.

By this time his hands are numb,
every wound and fissure burning wet salt.
You didn't see him heaving
tonnage from the writhing net
into the black hold again and again.

By this time the net is empty
except for a last hulking misfit,
this bastard blue.
You didn't see the fitful gasps
breaking from hundreds struggling.

By this time his brain is awash with private demons.
The image of her waltzing off
with that dry dock bum, you didn't see.

All you see is how Nate grabs that last fat one,
both hands on the tail
to fling its stupid water-logged head
whack into the smelly hold
along with all the other troubles.

All you see is Nate and his blue fish.

Thomas Peter Bennett
Silver Spring, MD

Memories

At breakfast, eating
strawberries from Florida—
March picking
with childhood cousins.
Who can pick the most
in five minutes?
Later,
the Florida Strawberry Festival
in Plant City.

At breakfast, eating
blueberries from Maine—
August picking
with wife and kids.
Who can pick the most
in five minutes?
Later,
in Machias,
the Maine Blueberry Festival.

***

Symbiosis

Downy woodpecker pecks...
tree bark and insects drop.
Cardinal swoops in...
pecks up the insects.

Susan Blackwell
Albuquerque, NM

Heaven-Sent Greetings

Since childhood, rainbows, balloons, and the sound of the neighborhood ice cream truck have always evoked a sense of joy and excitement. After losing my parents in the past few years, I've noticed those same sights and sounds bring comfort and peace when they arrive as heavenly messages from my mom and dad.

It may sound crazy, but I believe our local ice cream man was channeling a message from my deceased parents. It was the day before my birthday, and my husband and I were enjoying happy hour on our patio when we heard the ice cream man's nursery rhyme songs filling the air. After hearing *Mary Had a Little Lamb*, I was surprised to hear *Oh Susannah*, and laughingly said, "The ice cream man is playing my song." A moment later, when *Happy Birthday* rang out, my skin broke into goosebumps and I had an image of my mom and dad wishing me happy birthday from heaven.

For me, the significance and sequence of the songs, combined with my life-long romance with ice cream, heralded the arrival of a special delivery message. We could have assumed my imagination had gone into overdrive or that the happy hour margaritas were inspiring delusional thoughts, but I knew it was my parents because they have often communicated with me since they left this world.

Before my mom passed away in December 2017, my sister and I flew to Maine to be with her and my dad. During my mom's final days, we talked about family vacations, holiday memories, school days, and all the laughter and fun we enjoyed throughout the years.

We also shared our beliefs about the afterlife, and asked my mom if she could send us a sign when she got to heaven. Without hesitation, she promised to send a rainbow. When she passed away a few days later, my dad, sister, and I were

Susan Blackwell
Albuquerque, NM

thrilled when a beautiful rainbow appeared in the cloudless blue sky as we left the funeral home.

My dad also sent a sign from heaven when he made his final transition in April 2020. As I spent my dad's final four weeks with him, he told me how grateful he was for all the blessings in his life. He expressed his love for our family, his friends, his dog and best friend, Duncan, his travels, and his multiple careers. He was also grateful for all the books he wrote and published and for all his wonderful childhood memories.

I was surprised when he mentioned he had done everything on his bucket list except going for a hot air balloon ride. We agreed that's how he would travel to heaven, and we often laughed about this during our visits. Just as we asked my mom, I asked if he could send a sign when he got to heaven and he promised to send a balloon. The night after he passed away, *The Wizard of Oz* was on TV and my heart filled with joy when the hot air balloon appeared in the final scene.

Receiving my parents' heaven-sent messages has brought tremendous comfort as I grieved their loss. What's even better is their communication has continued, and always arrives at the perfect moment—reminding me that our loved ones are always with us and will remain in our hearts forever.

Bill Herring
Minnetonka, MN

Learning to Fish for Bluegills with Grandpa Rex

They stood together
at the end of the dock at Lake Ahquabi,
a peninsula of weathered wood
jutting out over the mysterious water.
He dipped his finger into a coffee can
filled with dirt, found a fat one,
slid it onto the hook, attached a
red and white bobber, then
cast about four feet out where
a bluegill convention was taking place
just below the surface.
He hooked one of the attendees
in front of the spiny dorsal fin,
reeled it in, then
let the slightly wounded fish swim free
before handing the bamboo pole
to his six-year-old grandson,
saying, *Here. Now you try it.*

I spent a good ten minutes taking aim
and casting, trying to impale the next fish
while Grandpa looked on, trying his best
to stifle his laughter.

Wendy Galgan
Boothbay, ME

False Dawn

Rice paper walls glow grey.
I wake the children,
bathe and dress them,
give them calming herbs
steeped in boiling water,
sing to them until they
drift to sleep in their chairs.

His letter waits on my dressing table.
Ebony on ivory tells me,
"No married man may fly."
Above it, he stares from a picture
sent from the air base.
Around his neck,
black ink on white silk,
he wears my name,
the name that prevents his flying.

I sit at the table,
reach up to twist my hair,
anchor it with combs—
ivory woven into ebony—
careful to keep my
movements slow, graceful
    in this, as in all things.

My hair in place, I don my
wedding kimono, adjust the
obi, slip on my sandals.
The light is tinged with gold now,
but dawn still has not come.
No birds call.

Wendy Galgan
Boothbay, ME

I wake the children,
lead them, drowsy and sweet-smelling,
one on each side,
back to the river that sings.
We step in. Silk rises to

billow about our ankles,
shins, waists.

The boy goes easily,
his hair slick beneath my palm.
The girl balks, looks up,
but bends to the hand at her nape.

I stand, one hand on each head,
count long minutes.
I wait to see them float.

At last I sit, ease back until the
riverbed presses between my shoulders.
The sun rises, a golden ball
between two dark shapes that
were my children.

My eyes open, I see a
silhouette against the sun.
My husband, grim-faced with joyful eyes,
at his plane's controls.

I drown so he may fly.

Joanne McNamara
Wells, ME

Stop and See

Stop and See
The beauty of the trees I bring to thee.
Hemlocks, birches, beech, and pines
Majestically overlooking the tines
Of the river that forks through the field below
Following its path, as if it knows its purpose.

Stop and See
This moment of serenity and breathe deeply.
Hear the ice melt as crystals cascade
To the frozen path that leads the way
In this journey called life on Earth
But savor this instant of rest on sweet turf.

Stop and See
And reflect on the greatness of you and just be
Thankful for everything under the sun,
Including the heartache, the sadness, and fun.
For without darkness we would not have light
That brings awareness and the sense of sight.

Stop and See
Look beyond the blue sky and see clarity
In clouds; their shapes change lackadaisically.
Knowing that patterns and cycles emerge
With the turning seasons which brings us courage
To face the unknown, whether friend or foe
Opening this mind and body to my soul.

Stop and See

Juliana L'Heureux
Topsham, ME

Imelda Had a Chapel

A group of American navy wives who were living at the Subic Navy Base in the Philippines, decided we wanted to visit the Malacañang Palace, in Manila.

This formal and sprawling estate is a lovely palace, situated where the vistas capture the Pasig River, in the nation's capital city. The Malacañang (pronounced mal-a-gan-yan) mansion, with the surrounding complex of buildings, is the official residence, and principal workplace of the president of the Philippines and the highest government officials. When we visited in 1974, it was the home of Imelda Marcos, who was the first lady of the Philippines when her husband, Ferdinand, was the country's president. They lived in the palace from December, 1965 to February, 1986.

Although Imelda is remembered for her vastly famous shoe collection, the fact is, she was also known to be a spiritual leader for the Filipino people. Her portrait was an icon adorning nearly every tiny home in the Philippine's barrios. Some people believed she lived a sort of double life, because, at home in the Philippines, she was more or less a self-appointed saint, but her extravagant shopping trips to Switzerland were notorious for over-the-top high-end retailing.

Nevertheless, her home at the Malaganang Palace was a beautiful historic mansion to visit because the landscape was a peaceful vista consisting of swaying palm trees and river views. We visited at a cool time of the year, during what we think of as being the fall, when the Philippine weather is usually ideal for travel because the rainy season is over. I was impressed by the number of stunning numbers of star-shaped parol lanterns blowing in the breeze, having been hung on the limbs in the trees.

Our wives' group consisted of about 25 spouses to navy

Juliana L'Heureux
Topsham, ME

personnel who were stationed at the Subic Bay Naval Base. We petitioned the Philippine authorities for permission to visit the palace, sort of like requesting a guided tour of the White House. Actually, it was quite remarkable for us to receive permission to visit, because the Philippines at that time was ruled under martial law during the 1970's, so the security was beyond belief tight. Our visit request may have been granted because of the many charitable works the wives supported through our international relief projects. For whatever reason, our request was granted.

Of course, the caveat was that we had to pass a very high level security clearance, even though we were already sponsored by the U.S. government. We were required to submit our passport information and to have a copy of our personal credentials with us when we visited. Moreover, the bus we traveled in was stopped about two or three blocks from the location of the palace, where armed soldiers entered to double check our names against the guest list. They also asked to see our passports, to verify the information we submitted with our permission list.

Eventually, after several walkie-talkie conversations in Tagalog between the guards with their security supervisors, the bus was allowed to proceed to the palace grounds. We were greeted by a handsome middle aged Filipino gentleman who was wearing an exquisite Barong Tagalog, the most formal of traditional men's wear, almost akin to an informal tuxedo. His presentation indicated to us that we were guests of honor. His English was perfect as he cordially explained instructions about our tour, including a short Malacañang history.

For example, Malacañan was the only major government building to survive the Battle of Manila, during very heavy artillery bombing in 1945, near the end of the Second World War.

My drama began just before we entered into the palace. The nice gentleman tour guide requested for us to please

Juliana L'Heureux
Topsham, ME

leave our purses at the security guard shack, located near the palace's entrance. We could pick them up when the tour ended. Whoa! Not so fast! All of us had our passports with us. Regardless of how cordial our host was, we knew better than to leave our purses with passports in the possession of the security guards. Therefore, like a Greek chorus, we politely declined. As a result of our understandable reluctance, he made one request. He asked us not to take any photographs inside the palace. Pictures taken outside were okay, but not inside. We agreed.

Although I joined in this agreement about no photographs, I had an old Kodak instamatic camera in my purse. Remember the hand held Kodak cameras where the flash cube was popped into the top? When a photo was clicked, the cube automatically circulated to the next flash. This rotation allowed four flash photographs to be taken without having to replace the cube. The only problem was, the flash, click, and rotation of the cube created noise.

We stepped into the formal entrance hall where the beige floors were made from Philippine marble. Then, we ascended the grand staircase to be shown the diplomatic reception rooms and the grand ceremonial hall, where dignitaries were received.

I was impressed with a particular lanai conference room, because it was a covered mezzanine, where one side opened out to a veranda and dozens of capiz-shell covered lamps hung from the ceiling lights. Breezes from the river caused the shells to create a soft wind-chiming carillon.

We were honored to be escorted into the private living quarters where Imelda and Ferdinand had created a music room and a library. Every room was decorated with what appeared to be royal decorum. Most surprising, was when we were allowed to visit Imelda's boudoir.

A value added experience was the privilege of entering Imelda's private chapel. Indeed, Imelda had her own devotional chapel, located in an antechamber that I recall being

Juliana L'Heureux
Topsham, ME

adjacent to her sleeping quarters. The idea, I suppose, was for us to experience how Imelda was devoutly religious, as demonstrated by how she quietly said prayers in her chapel, upon rising in the morning and before going to sleep. It seemed like the chapel was prepared to receive visitors. I have been on many house and castle tours, but never seen such a display of religiosity in a private boudoir! There were about three narrow rows of pews facing a small alter where the focus was a statue of the Virgin Mary, dressed like a folk doll wearing a black mantilla pieneta, veil and comb. Honestly, I was awestruck. Frankly, there are many thousands of images of the iconic Madonna Mary shrined in chapels, churches, basilicas and cathedrals around the world, but I doubt anyone will find a statue of the virgin wearing such formal Spanish traditional couture. At the foot of the statue was a cascade display of vigil lights, about 50 or so, all twinkling with real lit candles.

We were cramped in the small chapel, so the tour guide quickly moved us on to the next featured room. But, I quietly stayed behind. Certainly, no one would notice if I took one quick photograph of Imelda's chapel? Surely, the group would not miss me for a few minutes. Pulling the Kodak out of my purse, I lined the alter up in the lens and "snap," went the flash. Except, it didn't quietly go "snap." Instead, it went more like "ZZZZZnappp!" and the flash cube created an echo as it rotated. Horror of horrors, the echo reverberated into the hall where the group was congregating. It didn't take any longer than five seconds for the tour guide to find me trying to hide my camera back inside my purse. My heart stopped with fear. I could not imagine what he might do to me for taking a picture. *Surely,* I thought, *he would confiscate my camera.* And that's what he did, but in the kindest of ways. "Would you like for me to take a picture of you on the alter in Imelda's chapel?" he asked.

Well, I agreed, of course. At that point, I felt like throwing myself into Imelda's votive candles. He took my camera and

Juliana L'Heureux
Topsham, ME

he snapped a picture of me in Imelda's chapel. Then, he kept the camera, but with assurance that it would be returned to me when we exited our tour. He kept his promise. And, yes indeed, I thanked him.

Given the 21st century's super security, created to protect iconic places from surveillance, the incident with me in Imelda's chapel would probably not have ended with such a fondly memorable outcome, if my violation of the rules had happened in today's hyper-sensitive world.

What did I learn from my experience? It's difficult to say if I would even have remembered my visit to the Malacañang Palace, if it were not for my friendly scolding in Imelda's chapel. This rare experience can never be replicated.

As I reminisce, I am still impressed by the finesse our Philippine tour guide showed during this embarrassing moment. In fact, I silently thank him every time I see the picture he was kind enough to take, because he knew how awed I was by being in Imelda's private chapel.

Imelda Marcos had extravagant flaws with shoes and shopping. But, I have proof that Imelda also had a chapel.

Gerald George
Belfast, ME

Out of Order

The commandant of all the camps!
Coming here!
To see how we use our prisoners for the war!
All must be in order for his visit.
Dressed in our best uniforms,
each man stiff-standing to his task.
I welcome him myself.

Bring him to look over our books,
the daily numbers correct to the last man,
each one so many calories per day
so many days of labor 'til they die.
Everything measured with strict accuracy.
Surely for such precision in accounts
The chief will order promotions, even awards.

Then the chief pukes,
pukes on the death-house floor where the used-up go.
His aides tell me I needn't be concerned:
his is a "sensitive stomach," often upset.
Relief to me! I had felt cold fear
that he had taken offense, found something wrong,
something out of order in my camp.

P. C. Moorehead
North Lake, WI

Hearing

I hear the old voices,
calling me, imprisoning me.
I want to be free of them.
I want to roar:

"Take these old voices.
Take their sound
and change them,
transfigure them."

"Create for me a new voice,
a singing voice,
a free voice,
soaring to new life."

***

Deep

Swamp girl,
can you go deeper?
How far can you go before you sink?
How far can you go
before the mire claims you?

"I can go deep," I say.
"I can sink,
sink into power,
sink into mud,
and bloom."

Jean Biegun
Davis, CA

Shanties

What shall we do with a drunken sailor,
What shall we do with a drunken sailor,
What shall we do with a drunken sailor,
Early in the morning?

—Popular fishing shanty
(also spelled *chantey* or *chanty*,
from French *chanter: to sing*)

The shanties stagger all helter-skelter,
each thin wall straining under a drooping roof—
shacks thrown together with scrap wood,
bounded by wind-stripped weeds.

Fishermen there squat on land they don't own,
themselves stagger at dawn to the boats,
and sometimes one trips into grasping waves
and is gone.

Bright painted buoys are the men's trusted guides,
sun colors lighting their gray horizon,
sentinels for nets in pressing fog,
signs for the four directions and shore.

Golden-hued whiskey, amber siren of night,
lures them back through stars to home.
Staggering then from day-long labors,
they ache in every bone.

Tired of the stink of fish in their sweat,
ready to lift a jug, sleep near the stove,
they hope for easy dreams and drink
to the plucky ones who got out.

Graydon Dee Hubbard
St. George, UT

The Prize

The man rises early. Breakfast is brief but nourishing...eggs and oatmeal. He's exercising camping rituals not recently employed, but still present in treasured and time-worn memories.

Kneeling on a mantle of leaves, he rolls up an ageless down sleeping bag and frowns as he turns old grime stains into the curl. *Too imbedded,* he thinks. *Cleaning won't erase them.* Persistent aches in his legs and back remind him it's been a long time since he's used the ground as a mattress and his jacket for a pillow. He rises, stretches, combs his fingers through long, thinning white hair, and rubs some of the soreness out of his right thigh and hip. He's slept well enough. No troubled dreams. But he misses the companionship of a shared cup of coffee. After years of living alone, morning loneliness still pursues him, even here. Dark memories tarnish his thoughts. *Grime stains imbedded in my mind. Nothing will erase them either.*

Other, happier memories push aside the darkness. How long has it been? How long since he's last been here? Too long. He tries to remember the last time. He can't. Past events fuse in his mind, lack separateness.

He sighs and turns to listen to a far off murmur of moving water. Then, sounds from his past preempt the present. He remembers how the river gagged when rocks interrupted its flow, how it laughed when a narrows released it to riffle into a long and placid pool, how goldfinches trilled then twittered from streamside willows, how his father yelled "WHEEE—HAWW!" when he was into a good fish.

The man hopes the years haven't erased other memories. Will he still remember where the trout held, where they fed, what fly imitations he should use, how to present them, where the current ran too deep and strong to cross? He

Graydon Dee Hubbard
St. George, UT

wants to find again where the river surged straight and free through a treeless meadow. When you waded up the center, you felt weightless as the river swirled around your waist. A hundred yards of unmolested water beckoned to you from the sky's beginning. High grassy banks kept you captive in a long half-tunnel into timelessness where thoughts suspended pursuit and your mind emptied. You didn't think. You didn't need to think. You only reacted...with the river.

He feels apprehensive. Will the trout still be here? As fresh and colorful as he remembers? Can he really replenish treasured memories? Will the present confirm or deny his images from the past?

The man touches the ground, runs his fingers through some long blades of grass, and wipes the damp on his trousers. *Still wet with dew. I'm too early.* His eyes measure the sun's slow advance above the eastern horizon, and he smiles. *All day sunshine...maybe too bright?*

As he addresses the simple tasks of restoring his meager campsite and loading his rental car, he muses, *Why have I never brought my son here?* He'd always meant to. For each of many years he'd planned it, but always for the next year. And when the next year came? Always a reason why it couldn't be done and would have to wait another year. And now? It's too late. His son has long since left boyhood behind and now has a family of his own, with pressing responsibilities the man understands only too well. Disappointment lingers, a sadness that he's never brought to his son an opportunity to experience the enduring passion of his own youth. It's not a deep hurt, just a vague sense of something missing, an unfocused notion about what might have been. He feels close to his son, pleased with their relationship and the kind of person his son has become. But feelings of incompleteness nag at him. *A reminder of the many small failures everyone must acknowledge in a lifetime.*

Shrugging aside his temporary melancholy, he reminds himself he still needs a fishing license. A familiar restless-

Graydon Dee Hubbard
St. George, UT

ness...compulsion to be on the river and impatience with any delay...churns inside him as he turns the car back along his tracks from the night before.

At the nearby tackle shop, which also serves as gas station and post office, bustling activity has replaced the unhurried pace he remembers. Several hand-painted posters and a lineup at the cash register identify the cause. Derby day! The man winces as he shuffles to the end of the line. Unknowingly, he's selected the hamlet's annual trout derby for his brief journey into the past. *No matter,* he thinks. *It's years since I've cast to a rising trout and many more since I was here. My skills are rusty and my luck may be poor. It might be nice to find someone to talk to, perhaps even a familiar face. I can't expect to find the river as uncrowded as I remember it.*

As he waits for his turn at the register, he watches a group admiring the contest prizes displayed in a showcase to the side. Oblivious to those about him, a small boy, clean but raggedly dressed, leans against the case, his eyes riveted on the First Prize inside, a handsome bamboo fly rod. The boy's nose smudges the glass, and his breath clouds the surface. The man fancies he can see the longing in the boy's sad eyes. The rod nestles so close, yet so out of reach.

The boy is still there after the man secures his license. On impulse he stops to query the youngster, "That's a nice rod, son. If having it resulted from strength of wishing for it, I think it would be yours already. Have you signed up for the contest?"

"No, sir," the boy responds in a soft voice and polite manner. As he reluctantly turns his gaze from the prize, he looks at the man steadily and with curiosity for a silent moment before adding, "Bet you're a fisherman. You gonna enter the contest?" A blush of eagerness, not unnoticed by the man, follows the boy's question."

"No, son," the man answers. "I'm flattered you'd think me

a fisherman. But it's been a long time." *Too long,* he thinks. "Although I am going fishing, a competition isn't what I'd planned for today." The man senses the boy's eagerness turn to disappointment. He feels drawn to the lad, and, acting again on impulse before he can remind himself he's not an impulsive person, he adds quickly, "But, then...perhaps my plans aren't all that important. Maybe I will enter the contest."

Feeling a little foolish, but with his impatience somehow blunted by his conversation with the youngster, the man returns for a second wait at the register. When he finally reaches the counter, he turns, his eyes searching. The boy is gone.

The dirt road leading to the river curves sharply to the south and descends steeply into the valley. As he drives, the man feels a familiar excitement. Surprised he can still respond in this fashion, he wonders how this tantalizing anticipation can be so instinctively recalled after so many years and with the same intensity he'd experienced as a youth. *Only fishing produces this pre-sensation,* he thinks. *Except,* he smiles with recollection, *making love. I've abstained from both too long. Maybe both can be impervious to time.*

As he nears a grove of ancient cottonwood trees, he sees the familiar raggedy figure pedaling an old bicycle ahead of him. Slowing the car as he passes, he waves a greeting to his new small friend from the store and is rewarded with a quick smile of recognition. Thinking he should stop and renew the earlier conversation, the man hesitates. But his momentary indecision puts him into the cottonwood grove and out of sight. *Too late to follow his latest impulse. It's just as well. It's the fishing I'm here for. And the remembering. I should be alone.*

He stumbles when he eases into the edge of the river, and

Graydon Dee Hubbard
St. George, UT

he feels betrayed by uncertain steps and awkward casts. *Maybe time* ***has*** *taken its toll. Have I lost that much balance and coordination?* He waits for familiar wading and casting rhythms to reassert themselves. Cotton balls from riverside trees float like patches of foam on the surface before him, and he dabs at some with his rod tip, uses others as targets for casting practice. His confidence returns. So, his old skills aren't extinct, only dormant, saved somewhere in the recesses of his mind, waiting for memory and instinct to collaborate and renew them. They're the kind of skills one doesn't easily forget. Betrayed by a nervous tremble in his rod hand, youthful excitement is still his companion. His legs obviously aren't as strong or his reactions as quick, but his exhilaration feels as powerful as ever and raises his spirits. He chides himself for permitting so much time to slip by, for allowing matters perceived as too pressing to interfere and cause him to postpone a rendezvous with such an important part of his past.

After an unproductive 30 minutes of casting, the unaccustomed effort tires him. Turning to seek a rest on the bank, he sees his small new friend watching him quietly but intently from riverside. The boy smiles and waves. The man lifts his rod in salute. Feeling less tired, he returns to casting and promptly hooks a fish. Instinct takes over. The action is intense with lots of noisy splashing, both by the fish and fisherman, and the man soon nets a modest-size trout. He chuckles as he stifles the urge to announce his success with a war-hoop. *So it's come to that. An old man's dignity overcomes the sudden swelling of a more natural emotion. There* ***is*** *a boy still inside me.*

Again turning, the man smiles at the bright face behind him. "See young man," he says, as he releases the fish, "you bring me good luck."

The youngster, who's carefully followed every movement, lets his excitement overcome his un-boyish reserve. "Gee, mister," he exclaims, "you really are a fisherman." The boy's

Graydon Dee Hubbard
St. George, UT

eyes shine with expectation. "Hey, I know where there's a big trout. Just upstream," he points. "Under that tree. I climbed up there last week. Almost fell in when I saw him take something from the surface. Bet he's still there."

"All right, son, let's see if he is." The boy's enthusiasm is infectious, and the man ignores his fatigue as he lengthens his casts to reach under the tree. Overhanging branches reject or capture his efforts. "He's too well protected," the man calls to shore.

"Try from above," the boy instructs. "There's an opening you can float a fly into."

Repositioning 60 feet upstream, the man renews his presentation.

"That's it," the boy calls encouragement.

As the fly disappears into the opening, the man feels a barely perceptible line-tightening. Then a sudden, frenzied surface-thrashing announces a large trout's angry reaction to its mistake in identification.

This time dignity concedes to the emotion of the moment. "YAHOO!" The instinctive cry bursts from the man's lips. Again, "YAAAHOOOO!"

With an agility he's thought time would deny him, the man rushes downstream and toward shore, stripping line from his reel. "Here, son, you take the rod. It's your trout. You land him."

The rod falls into the boy's eagerly outstretched hands. "WOW!" he exclaims. His heart racing, the boy grips the straining rod with fierce determination.

"Ease up on him," the man instructs.

Under the man's expert guidance, the boy gradually relaxes and begins to regain line from the big trout. The boy's quickness, intense concentration, and obvious skill don't surprise the man. *The fish is more experienced, but the boy has the right instincts and a resolve that won't be denied. Reminds me of someone from long ago...me, I suppose, or how I'd like to remember my youth.*

Graydon Dee Hubbard
St. George, UT

Two figures laugh and stumble through the shallows, one gaunt and gesturing, the smaller sturdily guiding a rod now dancing with a wild creature's last surges for survival. The man blocks the trout's final dash for freedom with his legs, and then the boy backs up on shore to finally beach an exhausted and bewildered trout.

Spent but also refreshed from the exertion, the man helps the boy fashion a willow stringer for his catch. "There, son. That'll hold him. You take to it naturally. Better than any I've seen so young. Your first trout?"

"Yes, sir," responds the boy, returning the man's tackle, almost reverently. "Gee, I really caught him. Wait till I tell Mom. Thanks, mister." Delight shines in the boy's eyes, a mirrored reflection of the man's own.

"Here, son. Take the trout back to the store. He's a sizable fish and should bring you a prize. There's just time to meet the registration deadline."

This time a solemn "thank you" spreads over the boy's face...more eloquent than words. The man watches him pedal off, the big trout securely lashed by the willow wand to the handlebar basket, a wide tail spilling over the side.

After resting a few minutes, the man renews his fishing. A relentless ache of loneliness still pursues him, but less intensely. A feeling of accomplishment lightens his mood. He has difficulty understanding his thoughts. Uncertainty grips him. What's compelled him to return here? What did he expect to find here? The brief encounter with his new young friend has affected him...deeply. Impatience and compulsion are both gone. What's replaced them? He's unsure. Maybe a blending of contentment with serenity. He's actually at ease with himself.

He leaves the river at dusk, before the river's surface air can cool enough to chill him.

Curiosity prompts him to stop at the roadside store before heading to the airport. An empty prize-cabinet greets

Graydon Dee Hubbard
St. George, UT

him. “Excuse me,” he queries the store’s clerk. “Did a small boy, maybe ten years old, take a prize here today? Was he back in time to register?”

A broad smile crosses the clerk’s face. “Young Paul, you must mean. Yes, he was back in time. Had a prize-winner, too. Biggest trout caught today. Had to disqualify him though. He said someone else hooked the fish. Too bad when you have to reward honesty like that, but he knows the rules. Paul loves the river. Spends every Saturday here. Had his heart set on that rod, but there’s just no money at home for any decent tackle.”

Disappointed at first, but then brightening with a fresh thought, the man asks, “Do you have another, another rod similar to the prize?”

“No. Sorry. Only had one in stock. Don’t get calls for bamboo rods. Too expensive. No one appreciates classic rods any more.”

The man leaves the store and returns a moment later. Affectionately, he places his dismantled rod on the counter top. With a smile, he asks, “Here, would you wrap this up for Paul to pick up next Saturday? Please add a new reel and line to the package. Tell the boy it’s to thank him for what he did for an old man today. He’ll recognize the rod. There are more years of service left in that old bamboo than I’ll be able to enjoy.”

As he strides back to his car, there’s a new spring to his step, a fresh resolve in is heart. *Next year,* he thinks. *Next year I’ll come back. But not alone. For my son has a son, and it’s time he learned about rivers and how it feels to catch a trout.*

Robert B. Moreland
Pleasant Prairie, WI

Amber Waves

Across the vast amber expanse,
the wind conducts a ballet
and winter wheat dancers respond
to ancient music bittersweet.

To and fro, radiant synchrony
the masses perform unbridled,
firmly anchored by earthly roots;
alight in golden sunshine.

For I too am like winter wheat—
as from tiny seed to grow
and reach heavenward to dance,
a bliss life's bittersweet tune.

I know not when harvest comes,
dance of wind forever done.
Instead, I dance on God's time,
the best I can with all I have.

The life abundant is promised
in Him who danced through death—
yet, bore the ills of us all,
that we could dance with God.

Originally published as Moreland, R.B. (2013)
"Amber Waves" *The Bible Advocate* 147(2):25.

Donna DeLeo Bruno
Ft. Lauderdale, FL

Geniuses

Geniuses do not good husbands make.
Ask Mileva Einstein
Her husband Albert won The Nobel Prize
Solely he stood to accept it
For work they had done together.
Her mind as keen as his
Both students at the university
Her acute intelligence—a match for his.
Was promised equal partnership in scientific research
But pregnancy thwarted those plans.
Abandoned, she sought refuge with her family
But when summoned, went to wed in secret.
Their child—his child—succumbed to illness
Never acknowledged as their own.
Now instructed to walk steps behind him
Rage and bile rising in her throat
She yearned to scream—to tell the world
"**That** is **my** work too!"
Once famous and renowned,
He did not acknowledge her
No longer of any use to him.
Geniuses do not good husbands make
Ask Catherine Dickens
Whose talented husband penned masterpieces
Novels highly acclaimed in The Victorian Age
A Tale of Two Cities, David Copperfield, Great Expectations, Oliver Twist
With such compassion for the poor and orphaned
He made his readers cry for Tiny Tim, David and Oliver
Great was his empathy for the abused and downtrodden.
His long-suffering wife adored him—in awe of his talent.

(continued)

Donna DeLeo Bruno
Ft. Lauderdale, FL

She bore him twelve children
Depleted of energy, was relegated to a sanitarium
Her children forbidden to visit.
This author who tugged at your heartstrings
For the fictional characters he created
Had no heart whatsoever for his faithful wife.
Divorced, disowned her in the newspapers
A public humiliation.
Secluded her in some obscure attic space;
And still she forgave him all
Because he was a literary "genius."

Devoted and forgiving wives
Who gave their all
To men unworthy of their love.

***

Sylvia Little-Sweat
Wingate, NC

Birthday Wishes

From the start our hearts had
bargained love for more, but
like a burning coal your heart
held its own extinction. Did
your blood own its limits too
as it flowed through tubes to
a heart and lung machine that
pumped it back to you? Was
that why instead of cakes, I
baked you birthday pies from
apples so green and tart they
left us wanting sweeter fruit?

Mary Ann Bedwell
Grants, NM

Indian Winter

The mountains loom gray in the November dusk—
a skein of cloud covering the foothills
coalesces into a silent Indian band.

I kneel amongst the scree,
my hand on my dog's back,
(his hackles harsh against my hand)
a low growl leaves his throat.

No sound of hoofbeat or jingle of gear,
no bark of dog or cry of child.
The silent procession fades into the past.

Shaken, I wait,
hoping the mist will lift
and I will know what I have witnessed.

***

Sunrise at Arches National Park

You ask where have they gone,
the *Anasazi,* the old ones.
They are not gone, they are still here,
huddled in small groups, chatting,
the sun striking their morning robes.
They may glance at us,
small creatures skittering over the desert floor.
They pay us no attention.
We will soon be gone while they remain,
silent witnesses to the passage of time.

F. Anthony D'Alessandro
Celebration, FL

A Bilingual Boy Learns from Baseball's Best: Boys of Summer

First published in *Orlando Sentinel,* May 7, 2018

After sensing an "excuse me" knock, I pressed my ear against the front door. Abby, a former honor student stood there, swaying side-to-side like a hand-held fan. She said, "I'm back! I live in this complex now. Remembered your daily black coffee before class. Brought some." I hugged and thanked her.

"Come, sit on the porch. Everything okay?"

"Yes, Professor. I saw a video parading baseball altercations involving your favorite Yankee team. Just wanted your opinion."

"Altercations,"—great vocabulary. In my day we called them brouhahas or rhubarbs."

"I've never heard of those words," she said.

"Don't worry; it's not a sign of ignorance, just a barometer of age. I heard these words from early English instructors—baseball announcers."

She raised her brow. "Please tell me about that."

I described one of my days as a ten-year-old Brooklynite. After snatching my mom's radio from our plastic coated couch, I usually wriggled under her Formica table and plugged life into the radio.

I stretched out on the tile floor under the kitchen table, waiting to hear the echoing crack of baseball bats. That radio delivered a hidden Shangri-La. I twirled dials. After scratchy sounds, a clear signal touted the start of the game, and baseball broadcasters—my Boys of Summer—entertained me.

Scenes drifted across my mind. I pictured the immortal Jackie Robinson dancing on first base. Legendary Joe DiMaggio moved like an outfield gazelle. Broadcasters Vin Scully, Mel Allen, and Red Barber intrigued me. These gentlemen painted word pictures with the English language.

F. Anthony D'Alessandro
Celebration, FL

An American, born into an Italian-speaking family, I learned English from the Brooklyn streets, my school, and these announcers. Daily, I sprinted into my alley squeezing a Spaldeen (Spaulding) ball and mimicked words spoken by these famed radio raconteurs. I relished their soothing sounds whispering the nuances of baseball.

I don't recall bilingual programs or ESOL (English as a Second Language) teachers during my boyhood Brooklyn days. Those baseball mentors never strolled into my schoolrooms to teach me English. Yet, they conducted a classroom on my childhood radio.

I imitated. Pretending to be Red Barber, I sat in his imaginary "Catbird Seat." I did not have the faintest idea what it meant. It sounded cool, so I repeated it. On other days, I emulated Mel Allen's "How about that!" chant. I frequently echoed Vin Scully's description of "high drives."

Their picturesque ball yard tapestries left me with mouth agape. I choked the end of a baseball bat wrapped in electrical tape. It became my fake microphone while I spoke into the bat handle. Standing between red brick walls of two muscular homes, I tossed the ball and announced my fantasy game. Sportscasters Allen, Barber, and Scully groomed my imagination and speech. I patterned my words to their rhythms.

Sadly, Allen, Barber, and Scully are gone. Scully, my only remaining mentor recently retired his microphone. All that's left of my mentors are memories of velveteen voices whispering in my reverie, thoughts of faded family, and Brooklyn summers. Thanks to the invisible conductor named radio, I learned from these word wizards. They delivered suitcases packed with baseball dreams and the melodious lyric of the English language.

"Wow, Professor," said Abby. "I came to talk about baseball altercations and learned a vibrant piece of living history. I'm sure those Boys of Summer taught millions of others too. Thanks for sharing."

Matt Bernier
Pittsfield, ME

The Unfinished Business of Winter

I hated to see winter end outside my kitchen window,
lines and margins etched in blank pages of snowy fields
as muddy deer tracks pressed into clay like hieroglyphics,
purple finches spilling into feeders like purple prose,

harsh consonants sung in the rain as they flung seed
around only to blossom as prickly thistles in summer,
and in the woods the sappy maples wept from injuries
of ice storms and missing limbs, only to be edited into

something sticky and sweet when spring was published;
I have unfinished business with this particular winter,
words unspoken when a piece of tamarack in a fireplace
popped and showered sparks beyond the brick hearth

as my guest flinched, then leaned closer and laughed,
and now, in the judgment of longer days I think of the
snow-covered roads that kept us together that evening
as an empty composition book, no one making a mark.

Bonnie L. Ewald
Brooks, ME

Schoodic Point

In this ancient land of loon and sea, diamonds spark atop
the waves.
Burnt Sienna rocks jet out into the rippling abyss.
Dark Umber crevasses break through heavy boulders,
Reflecting yesteryear, and many roads not taken.
Wild roses nestle in their embrace, sheltered from the many
storms.
Rays of Flake White sun streak through Payne's Grey skies,
Dropping like shards of glass into the sea.
White salty spires of foaming spray crash into the ledge.
A great white fin rises from the sea, and just as quick,
Disappears to his Prussian Blue labyrinth below.
Colorful gum drop buoys merrily bob along the shore.
A seal pops up his head, looks frantic, and disappears.
Memories fade over the long ride home as
Raphael angels peek through the windows of the darkening
clouds.

***

Patrick T. Randolph
Lincoln, NE

A Poem of Thanks

One brief word from you,
Even a simple nod of your head—
And my soul can't help but
Soak itself in smiles.

Alice Oldford
Lake Placid, FL

Pandemic at the Lake

It was a quiet Monday morning on Little Sebago Lake, a perfect day for kayaking. The clear, cool water sparkled under the sun's rays. I removed my mask and gulped a lung full of fresh air. Then I was off to enjoy what the lake had in store. The fish shimmer as they jump hoping to capture an insect. The sound of the water lapping the shore soothes my soul. A large snapping turtle suns himself on a huge rock which protrudes from the lake. You may have heard of walking meditation. Why not kayaking meditation?

I was looking for loons without success. I did see a man waving his arms and shouting at ducks crowding his dock. He was not particularly successful since the ducks were not bothered. I opted out of range of his vitriol as quickly as I could manage.

As I paddled toward another cove, I was distracted by a squirrel hanging upside down on a bird feeder gobbling as much seed as possible. A fellow squirrel chose not to climb and picked up whatever fell to the ground.

I heard a gentle hooting sound a mama loon makes to keep the chick from wandering too far. When I turned, a loon family was swimming nearby. There were two other kayakers in the area. Mama and papa loon dove and each returned with a fish for the chick. One of the other kayakers brought out a camera with a long lens and photographed the feeding.

A bystander on shore told us we just missed an eagle considering the chick for lunch. The chick dove, and the parents literally stood up to the eagle, flapping, sounding the tremolo warning alarm, and preparing to spear the predator threatening their chick. The eagle did not risk the loons' wrath and flew off to seek an easier meal. The moral, do not threaten a loon family.

I paddled on and found a great blue heron wading along

Alice Oldford
Lake Placid, FL

the shoreline, stalking lunch.

I love this time of year at the lake. The air is crisp with a hint of wood smoke. The vacationers have left town, no boat wakes to dodge. The red sugar maples suggest an imminent fall. I am counting my blessings.

I came back from a leisurely paddle with a smile, a clear head, and a renewed appreciation of nature's offerings. What a relief to talk about something other than pandemic woes and quarantine. Tomorrow I think I'll look for an eagle's nest.

***

Joanne McNamara
Wells, ME

Listening to Fog

Flapping of wings as ducks take off from the water
Chirping of the bald eagle in search of fish
Fish jumping as if to say "come and get us"
The slight purr of hummingbird wings in the nearby
flowerpot
Cawing crows antagonizing eagles and humans
Intermittent dripping as the fog droplets meet tree leaves
Buzzing bumblebees looking for nectar
Frolicking squirrels making their clicking sounds,
beckoning others to play
Car wheels on gravel and a beep of the horn, signaling
departure of family
Propeller plane engine overhead carrying passengers to, and
then from, Owls Head
The long blast of a distant horn, saying beware
As the fog lifts, sounds diminish and are absorbed into the
day.

Grace B. Sheridan
Cutler, ME

Lakeside

Come,
lounge with me
on the deck with sips
of wine and conversation
while woodpecker nips
at suet bag and chipmunk
scouts for crumbs.

Come,
stroll with me
to the dock secure
in green-edged cove
where beaver have begun
to strip another maple tree
for their stick-built home.

Pause with me,
silent as deerskin moccasins
between the towering trees,
search for source of bird-sung hymn,
follow the columns to arching limbs
where leaves tat lace with sunlit thread
and sough a lakeside song.

Sarah Woolf-Wade
New Harbor, ME

No Lights in the Windows

No lights in the windows
from the house next door.
Snow flies sideways
out of the northeast,
freezes along the shore.
Old homes loom
dark and empty.
In former years this was a road
glowing with warmth.
What happened to turn it around in time
to wintry gloom and snowy silence?
Where did they go—
the piano player, singers,
fiddlers, storytellers—
clustered together in winter
sharing their lives with laughter?
Gone. All gone.
Winter warmth frozen away.

Later this spring,
strangers will come
with vacation toys, kayaks,
nannies and bikes,
grownup children
on two-week breaks
from busy city careers.
Some rent to others,
ignoring us all.
Some prowl the shoreline
to tear down old homes
and rebuild anew.

(continued)

Sarah Woolf-Wade
New Harbor, ME

Some of us will survive,
winter people
in a summer place,
alone.

***

Karyn Lie-Nielsen
Waldoboro, ME

Change of Heart

A bird flies in your window
builds a nest
in soft branches,
the fertile arbor,
garden of your heart.
After a few arched flutters
changes start.
In sharper light
feathery flakes part
like elements
of rough shells, hard
and tuneless.
Your heart is now
arid and windy,
chambers scarred
where infant birds marred
the feeble bars
before deciding
it was time to depart.

Kaye Nelson Ratliff
Wadesboro, NC

The Art of Taking a Walk, Rain or Shine

First, wake up early and stick your head out the door
to check the weather—then
dress accordingly. If it looks like rain, grab an umbrella.
Raining hard? Stay home and grab a good book.
Pocket a few treats for the cats and dogs you'll meet,
making friends with those who don't run away.

Take note of the trees and shrubs
you meet as well. Give them
names if you want, the Grandfather and Grandmother
oaks, the Southern Belle magnolias, the Everlasting
Majesty pines. Learn from them,
how they share their food and shelter their young.
Take a magnolia blossom for a June wedding, some pecans
for a Thanksgiving pie, a red camellia and a holly branch
to grace your Christmas table. And don't forget
to say a word of thanks.

Inhale the scents that mark the season. Step close
to smell the delicate perfume of mimosa and marvel
at the sweet aroma of the shrub that blooms only in the
fall.
Listen for the birdsong and how it changes through the
year—
except the mockingbird, of course—ending with the
cacophony
of crows and jays.

And always, always lift your face to accept the wind.
Who knows, it might be
the breath of God.

Rev. Deborah Loomis Lafond
Raymond, ME

Christmas Messenger

I was startled when I saw tracks in the snow that seemed to have magically appeared. I'd pulled up the window shades only minutes before, and marveled at how the fresh snow covering the lake resembled white hospital bed sheets of days long ago, laundered and pressed, crisp and dazzling. I shielded my eyes from the glare but lingered nonetheless to appreciate the simplicity, clarity and serenity of the sight before me.

"White Christmas this year," I said turning away from the window as my husband, Arthur, entered the room. When I resumed opening the curtains, I saw tracks that had not been there just seconds before. They seemed to start...where? There was just a straight line of them. But wait. What was that indentation alongside the footprints? It looked like someone was trailing a stick. I reached for the binoculars that we keep on the window sill. Lakeside living provides the best free entertainment from nature and in the summer, from people, too!

Eyes focused, I nearly dropped the glasses. About 20 feet from shore (no more than 60 feet from me) was a Canada goose walking sprightly along the snow covered ice where only days before, it had been swimming. "Odd," Arthur and I mused to each other, that the bird wasn't flying; must be cold on its webbed feet and not good for them.

Simultaneously we gasped, each of us seeing the goose's right wing hanging by its side. We heard weeks before that a bird had been injured, its wing torn from its shoulder. Now the creature was passing in front of our house, valiantly dragging its hideously wounded wing.

Each of us reached for our technological tools—I for my cell phone, he for his tablet. We were sounding an alarm to our neighbors, the other year-rounders who brave the four seasons on the lake and look out for the variety of lifeforms that make residing here so rich. Reports of the bird were texted, posted on Facebook, and left on answering machines.

The prospects of helping the goose were unlikely but because lake dwellers care deeply about wildlife, they would go to great lengths to save it. Its story of survival was amazing. Its desire to live, inspiring. It had been able to sustain itself on the water for eight weeks, but in its vulnerable condition now it was a wonder that an eagle hadn't attacked it. Anyone who'd seen the ailing goose made that observation.

So Arthur and I lifted up prayers to the patron saints of creatures great and small—to St. Francis, St. Columba, and of course, St, Nicholas. After all, it was the week before Christmas.

People in the area contacted several potential sources of help who advised the same thing: gently cover the goose with a blanket and as carefully as anyone could, place it in a large dog crate. Then transport the animal to a shelter or call someone from Inland Fisheries and Wildlife to come for it.

Neighbors nearby reported seeing the goose cross Hayden Bay where it found respite on Hill Island. The lake had frozen over only the week before so no one was going to risk walking on thin ice to reach the island. We lamented. With the temperatures well below freezing and diminished food sources on land, we knew the creature could not live much longer. Facebook postings agreed, "All we can do is pray."

Despite their love of nature, I didn't expect the outpouring of people's concern because property owners around the lake always complain about Canada geese congregating on their lawns, fouling them, leaving behind parasites, and swimming in large flocks that create hazards for swimmers and boaters. Nevertheless, many expressed hope for a miracle rescue of this brave bird now rendered a pitiful creature.

Midafternoon on December 24, I was distracted by a shadow moving across the lake. Standing in the same spot

Rev. Deborah Loomis Lafond
Raymond, ME

where I'd first seen the goose tracks in the snow, I now saw an eagle flying very low, struggling to carry a heavy load. Through the binoculars, I saw the carcass of the goose in its talons. I felt sad, but I felt my face muscles working to hold back the smile forming on my lips. Then I let the "Alleluia! Thank you!" burst forth. I was grateful that the goose's suffering was over, its spirit released.

There is a Christmas legend about how each year, God sends angels to earth close to the time of celebrating Christ's birth. God wants to find out how human beings have incorporated Christ's messages of hope, peace, joy and love into their lives, how they have used the Christmas message to make life better for others. The legend focuses on one angel whose task is to bring back a sign that God's love is still alive on earth. I like to think of that Canada goose as the Christmas messenger who felt the goodwill of people whose compassion towards it was greater than their contempt. I like to think that an angel in the form of a Canada goose heard the prayers of the lake dwellers and knew it had completed its assignment. The Christmas messenger would tell God about the caring it experienced as an injured goose, and of the warmth of prayers that helped it survive while bringing neighbors together for love's sake.

***

Dying into the Light

Let me die at the end of the day
When the waning light
Heralds the continuation of the journey
From light into light.
On the other side of the world,
A new morn is dawning
And with it, the possibilities of peace.

Hans Krichels
Bucksport, ME

Sandman in Acadia

(Day #255 of this Pandemic in Our Town)

Magnificent! The shoreline, the mountains,
Great Head in the background.
Far away, the great pandemic of 2020 rages
through the countryside.
It is late October now in Acadia National Park.
The beach is deserted—except for me (or so it appears).
Just below, someone has expertly carved a figure
into the sand,
a paunchy, middle-aged man with jowly cheeks
and balding head,
sprawled on his back: Every man awaiting his fate.
I stand, just above the figure's head, watching the waves
roll in, lap at his feet.
Time and tide, they say, for no man wait.
Like sand through an hourglass, the toes wash away.
A swirling of frothy water, and the feet are gone.
Standing a bit farther back now, I document this process
with my Canon EOS 1000.
Fugacia omnia, I think to myself, as the ankles
and knees disappear.
Yes, all is fleeting, I repeat, but this at least I will preserve,
a creation of my own, overriding the best intentions of the
artist before me.
I capture the rounded belly as it dissolves into smooth
glistening sand.
And then, oh so smug in my godliness,
I look up and see to my left, high on a ledge on the
path to Great Head,
a man with a tripod and a camera like my own,
capturing his own story of me and the story I am telling.

(continued)

Hans Krichels
Bucksport, ME

I look back to the figure at my feet. Only the tips
of the ears remain
and the crescent dome at the top of the head.
I step back from the rising tide, the waves swirling and
lapping at my feet.
Above me, the man on the ledge has vanished.
It is only me now...and the gentle washing of the waves.

***

Gerald George
Belfast, ME

So Many People

. . . piled into the sorting camp from different cities, waiting for the next train out, days sometimes, trying to make sense of it, the well-dressed elderly woman who didn't want to share her bunk with somebody from a slum, or the beauty queen who set up her compact mirror on a crate to do her eyebrows before she had to go elsewhere, or the middle-aged man in tears, sitting haphazardly in mud, his wife and daughters already gone while they held him for some kind of work, or the old woman asking if she could go home to fetch her medicine bottles —oh, yes, and her new spectacles— could she go now? No? Where were they taking her? Why, why, why . . . ?

Susan Sklan
Cambridge, MA

Believing Adults

My mother sewed me gold taffeta wings
and told us there was no such word
as *can't.*
My sister and I took off from there.
We wrote messages, stuffed them in empty bottles
and tossed them off the cliff.
Peacocks once lived on the land now our garden.
We would search for their feathers
and dig for gold coins that were rumored
buried near the mulberry tree.
After the rain we collected snails and stuck them
to the window to trace their silver paths
and every year we caught Christmas beetles
with their iridescent wings
before they stripped the peppercorn tree bare.

We were given proof over and over
that life was charmed.
Once a tomb was open in the cemetery down the road.
We held hands as we dared to look inside
and were able to run home
before anything evil burst loose.
Everything my sister lost was returned to her—
her dog, her colored pencils,
and I wasn't hurt when I fell out of the swing
that hung from the branch that snapped.
All this, before we learned about loss and betrayal.

Philancy Comeau
Rockland, ME

Paradise in Ashes

Perhaps it was a dream, Loretta thought. Perhaps if she pinched herself, she would wake up. But she didn't want to wake up. She wanted to stay in this dream world where her life remained unchanged for twenty years after leaving the city and her life-consuming work in the world of finance as a hedge fund manager.

The Sawatch Range of the Colorado Rockies is where Loretta lived for those twenty years as one with land and beast instead of money and beast. That was until July 4, 2009, when the Firecracker Forest Fire ate its way across her property. It gobbled up everything on its plate except her small cabin home and a few spotty stands of trees. These items pushed to the side were left scarred but alive.

Instead of the emptiness of humanity, she felt the void of nature burned to ashes. The fire consumed the forest's soul, like the world of finance consumes a person's soul. Only the strongest are left standing to thrive again.

Days after the fire, she stood on her back porch, numb to the loss of the life she loved. Everywhere she looked, she saw jagged, black needles poking into the pale blue sky, accenting the harshness of her surroundings. The usual crisp, fresh air was now flat and warm. The odor was unbearable as it seeped into her body through her breaths and pores. The effect worsened by the once soothing breeze. First, she wondered if this is what it would be like to live in a giant ashtray. Then she saw herself flying coach in the smoker's section back in the day on a never-ending nightmarish flight. Across the landscape, boulders once covered with lichen were left scarred, sitting on a dimpled surface similar to a golf ball. The fire reached deep into the loam, digging for fuel like a child searching through a bowl of M & M's for the last of their favorite color. The golf ball-like surface made walk-

Philancy Comeau
Rockland, ME

ing through most of her land nearly impossible.

She glanced down the hill behind her cabin. What she saw brought instant nausea; she quickly looked away. The pristine water she counted on for subsistence of spirit and body became tinted by the runoff of rainwater sliding down the hillside and into the lake. The once teardrop-shaped lake, the color of her aquamarine birthstone pendant, had turned the color of the pavement she left behind in the city.

When she dared to venture away from her cabin, she came across bones of moose and mule deer that couldn't outrun the flames or were trapped by their racks in a dense grove of trees. She cringed at the fright of the animals in their last moment of life before the fire's teeth bit into them and swallowed hard. The most devastating loss of sound and soul from the fire were the vanished songbirds and raptors. Their departure left the forest darker than the charcoal of the trees and the ash of the loam.

After the fire, life on her property was impossible. The impacts forced her to leave her home and search for paradise elsewhere. She never lived surrounded by nature again. Instead, she found nirvana in the heart of a man where she lived happily for many years, a heart whose time had come and gone in the same way as her land. Both were once alive and vibrant, then died and turned to ash.

At the end of her life in a nursing home, Loretta lies helpless in a fire-resistant forest of shiny metal cabinets, white uniforms, and plastic gadgets owned by a faceless hedge fund. The paradise she found in nature and then the human heart left her never to return, except in her dreams. She longs for darkness to come from within and for the promised nirvana to be again.

Charles Fletcher
Montville, ME

A Vector

You, my dear, terrible Vector,
Arrow that's longing for blood,
Release yourself, through empty air,
Toward a target of canvas and wood.

Or, is it I who shoot myself,
Deep in my wooden heart,
Walk around, foolishly, dripping,
And wait for the sirens to start?

***

Labor Day

Recalled, my limbs re-rivet themselves
Into their proper places. (That one's not mine,
I think.) Still, I miss being parted out
Over the mudflats: after the gulls let go,
Floating on the air, 'til the crack of rock,
Breaking me, wake me, over and over.

Elizabeth Lombardo
Walpole, ME

Moonrise Over Pemaquid

Faces bared to the salty wind
We stand on ancient ground
Revelers nestled among the rocks
Waiting, backs toward the glow of sunset's red
Rosy, golden against the blueness of freshest night
Eyes drawn to the darkness of endless water.
The chill reminds us we are still alive
As we wait in silence
Captivated like the tide
Drawn to the perfect orb as it rises in quiet glory
And then, the reflection
Hauntingly beautiful on this mystical night
Like the River Styx, illuminating the depths of countless
souls
Ever increasing, matching emotions deep within
The path elongates into the darkness.
Visible beauty fading into the allure of the unknown
The peace that surrounds us is palpable
The quiet despite the tumult of the waves
The stillness despite the trembling of the hands
Close by your side, I feel day shift to night.
Even the sea cannot fathom
The unearthly expanse that lies between us.

Sylvia Little-Sweat
Wingate, NC

On the Map

In early trapping days in Union County,
beavers felled trees with their sharp front teeth
then dammed the creeks with log jams.

Named Beaver Dam Creek on survey maps,
the creek still serpentines through woods and fields
past a town first called Beaver Dam.

A handwritten deed bequeathed land four miles
hence "on the waters of Beaver Dam Creek"
to Willis Pinkney Pierce and his wife Sarah.

Pierce descendants tilled the fields for more than
a hundred years—raising corn for mules and pigs
and cotton to be picked by hand then hauled to the gin.

The town's name in time was changed to Marshville.
Even before the four-lane bypass, the Carolina
Railway had split downtown into Main and South Main.

The old livery stable and the tin cotton gin
gave way to drive-in banks, barber shops, and Bojangles,
but since the fifties the Wagon Wheel Grill has survived.

It first stood opposite the cotton gin—a graveled drive-in—
but now it serves Regulars inside hamburgers and fries
with copious sides of nostalgia and small town gossip.

Linda Amos
York, PA

In the Company of Friends

She enjoyed the quiet
   As she walked with her old dog,
At a slower pace now, giving her more time
   To catch up on her prayers.
Praying blessings upon those
   She liked and those she loved.
Both she and her dog would return home
   Not so much exhausted but as weary.
Walking with her old dog was an ordeal,
   Now that his eyes had dimmed.
His trust-in-her, his lifelong companion;
   Compounded her appreciation of him.
They were after all, old friends,
   Grateful for another day of each other's
companionship.

***

P. C. Moorehead
North Lake, WI

The Cart

Pushing into the future,
pulling the past behind—
push-pull, push-pull—
pulsh.

Pulsh,
the tension holds—
emptying, filling—
The balancing act of grace.

Alfred Kildow
Boothbay Harbor, ME

The Flyboy

There were old pilots and there were bold pilots.
But no old, bold pilots, until...

The sky overhead was suddenly crowded with piston-powered airplanes, old ones, a few nearly a century old. Their roar filled the senses.

It puzzled the old man, standing on the grass outside his suburban Dallas home. He looked quizzically at his neighbor, a younger man, maybe 75 or so, standing not far away on his own lawn.

"Commemorative Air Force," the neighbor said. "A bunch of old veterans flying around to celebrate Memorial Day."

The old man nodded, then said: "I used to fly, you know. Korean War." He pointed to a tight formation, four planes growling low over the subdivision. "Flew one of those. T-6. First plane I ever flew. First plane I was ever in. I'll never forget that old T-6...."

But the neighbor had turned away and gone inside. He had war stories of his own but never told them. He'd spent his entire army service in El Paso.

In the newspaper the old man learned that the flock of old planes had come from far and wide, gathering together nearby at the airport in Addison from which their pilots launched their tribute. A few days later he drove his 20-year-old Chevy over to see if any T-6's remained. To his delight, one did.

The old man strolled over to the T-6, walked all the way around it twice, then caressed the bright yellow-orange fuselage with his calloused hands, stepped back a few strides to continue admiring it.

"It's a T-6," a voice behind him said suddenly. "A trainer first used in World War II. You ever seen one before?"

The old man turned to face him and said, "Yeah, I have.

Learned to fly in one, back in '49." He studied the man carefully, calculated he was no older than 50, maybe younger.

The old man stuck out a paw, introduced himself. Then added: "My buddies back in the day used to call me 'Motormouth.' Buddies in my squadron. Back then."

The younger man replied without emotion. "I own this plane. Bought it a couple years ago. Fly it when I have time, usually two or three times a month."

"When I flew it," the old man said, "we flew two or three times a day." He laughed as he said it, looked away, let his glance linger on the sturdy-looking monoplane, leaning back to rest on its tail wheel.

The two talked enough for the old man to learn that most of the time the T-6 just sat there at the airport, occasionally drawing wondering attention from a passersby.

"I was about to go on a short hop about the area," the younger man said. "Want to ride along?"

The old man felt his heart leap. "Sure would. Been a long time since I flew this kinda bird. Any kind. Would feel mighty fine."

He climbed into the back seat on instructions from the owner, who said he'd do the flying; the old man would just ride along. After he managed to scramble into the back seat, he found it comfortingly familiar. On the seat was a parachute that also served as a cushion, just as he remembered. He strapped himself in automatically, pleased he remembered the process so easily. Studied the instrument panel, found it simple, easily understandable, much less complicated than the last panel he'd been required to scrutinize, sometimes urgently. More recently than in T-6 days but still a long time ago.

He tugged the headset from where it hung on the rearview mirror, heard a crackly "Read me?" in the earphones, pressed the mic close to his lips and gave it his best veteran response: "Uh (pause) roger."

The owner was effusive and generous, although the old

man rated him only adequate as a pilot. He answered his many questions fully and directly. It seemed to the old man that just as he formulated a question the answer came to him, always a second or two before the younger man answered. Mostly his questions had to do with mixture and pitch. When to lean or enrich the gasoline to air mixture, how to position the pitch of the propeller, how to vary it for takeoff, cruising or landing. He'd once known all of that without thinking about it but the jet fighters he'd mostly flown had no reason for him to remember that nonsense. The jet fighter was just, an instructor had told him years ago, "a hole sucking air, then squirting it out back on fire."

The owner flew around the Dallas area for nearly an hour, mostly cruising along straight and level, taking in the scenery. "Want to take over the controls for a bit?" he asked over the intercom. "Hey, yeah," came the quick reply. "I mean, roger," he said with a thumbs up gesture that only he could see.

He could feel the pulsed vibration of the big radial engine when he grasped the stick, felt its familiar shape, tickled the trim tab button atop it, wiggled the trigger like scratching an itch, chuckling to himself, imagining the trigger was connected to something powerful, meaningful, knowing it wasn't.

He flew around for ten or fifteen minutes, cruising, mimicking the straight and level flying of the owner, risking only gentle turns, gradually heading further out into the western countryside, chatting amiably over the intercom with the younger man in the front seat. Over an area where there were few houses, the old man asked, "Mind if I try a chandelle?"

"What's a chandelle?"

"Oh, just a simple training maneuver. First one I learned as a cadet. They called it a 180-degree maximum performance climbing turn. Not a big deal. Just dive a bit to get some airspeed, power up, then turn and climb at the same time."

Alfred Kildow
Boothbay Harbor, ME

He had, of course, executed that same maneuver thousands of times over his years on active duty, not usually thinking about it or its name. With the power of "air on fire" it was just a routine way to turn around.

Before the owner could reply, the old man pressed the stick forward gently, added some power and let the airspeed build up. At 250 knots he pulled the stick back and pushed the throttle full forward at the same time. Rolling briskly into the turn he heard the younger man grunt as the G-load built up. The G-force didn't bother the old man. He'd tightened his gut with reflexive anticipation as he rolled the old T-6 into the steep climbing turn.

"I'll take it," he heard the owner command, hearing his frantic shout both in the earphones and over the subduing roar of the engines as he yanked the throttle back and took control. "That's too violent for an old airplane like this."

The old man in the back seat didn't think so but said nothing. The old bird had reacted just the way he'd expected it to. Smooth and precisely responsive, just as it had for him a few thousand flying hours before. A thousand years, it seemed to him.

They parted amiably enough, there on the tarmac at Addison airfield. He rubbed his hands again over the metal fuselage, watched the tanker truck arrive and the gas boy refuel the plane. He stopped for a moment, alongside his car in the nearby parking lot, studied how the owner fastened down a canvas contraption to protect the Plexiglas cockpits of his T-6.

The old man started up his Chevy and headed for home. "Eighty," he said aloud. "That bird's 80 years old." He laughed at that. "And this old bird's 90. Two old friends."

***

It took him a month to get up the nerve. But early in the dark of morning the old man parked his Chevy again at the airport in Addison, something he had done in that same spot a handful of times since his ride in the T-6.

This time he got out of the car.

The old man walked purposefully to the T-6 and removed the canvas cover, folded it carefully, set it down near the fence. He yanked away the chocks that blocked the main landing gear, climbed up on the wing, then paused. He looked at the runway, it's lights gleaming in the distance. Too far, he thought.

A taxiway led from the T-6 to the runway. A hundred yards away, at least, he thought. The air was still. The tower closed. No one about.

In five minutes the old man had the T-6 in the air, rising from the taxiway, wheels and flaps pulled up before crossing over the runway. He flew low over the full expanse of the airport, building up speed. At 200 knots, chandelle! From south to north in less than a minute, then a gentle climbing turn to the west, leveling off at 5,000 feet with the rising sun reflecting in the rear view mirror. It was eight o'clock and beneath him the land was brightening up, streets and buildings coming into view.

He looked about carefully, making sure no other aircraft were in the area. He unfolded his map, an old WAC chart of the West Texas area on which he'd made numerous notations.

The old man grinned, spoke aloud in a whisper: "It may not work. They may catch me. But this sure is fun."

A half-hour later he circled over the little town of Haskell, picked out the schoolyard where hundreds of children milled about. He could see a group kicking a ball, others running haphazardly. Most looked up to the sky, expectantly, he told himself. He eased the throttle back, pointed the nose toward the schoolyard and went into a steep dive.

A quarter mile from the schoolyard he leveled off at 50 feet, pushed the throttle up and banked slightly, pointing the nose so that he passed just off to the side of the schoolyard.

Alfred Kildow
Boothbay Harbor, ME

With the throttle wide open and the engine roaring the T-6 sped past the school at 250 knots. He looked over to the side and saw the children standing stock still, mouths agape, some running around excitedly, pointing at him.

Chandelle! Then another turn and a dive for a second pass. Children waving, jumping up and down. He pulled up just short of the school, and not fully realizing what he was doing, executed a perfect barrel roll. He circled back at 2,000 feet, waggled his wings, climbed back to 5,000 feet and resumed his trek to the west.

A half-hour later he repeated his airshow at the town of Seminole. It was morning recess, just as he'd calculated, and the schoolyard was full. His five-minute performance was clearly appreciated, at least by the children, whom he watched jumping up and down and waving, just like the kids at Haskell. His heart felt full.

Well before noon, right on his schedule, after two more performances, he landed at the airport just south of Roswell, New Mexico, taxied over to the row of private aircraft hangers. He pulled up to where an attendant was motioning to him, guiding him to park alongside a fuel truck.

"Welcome, sir. Got your reservation. We'll fill you up quickly, like you asked."

The old man climbed down, stretched and accepted a boxed lunch from the attendant, tucked it under his arm.

"Well, sir, I hear you put on quite a show over there to the east," the attendant said. "Folks in the hanger were talking about it just a bit ago. Hope you didn't break any rules."

The old man smiled, said nothing, paid cash, climbed back into the cockpit. He watched the fuel cap screwed back on and looked off toward the tower. He stiffened. A police car was headed his way, seemed to him to be moving fast.

He fired up the engine, watched the attendant scurry away, a bewildered look on his face. Power on full, flaps at 20 degrees, he rolled down the tarmac pointed directly at the speeding police car. It swerved away at about the same instant the old man yanked the T-6 into the air, simultaneously pulling up the landing gear. He got a quick look at a terrified policeman glaring at him from the patrol car.

Much too close, he mused as he headed north, climbing again to 5,000 feet, his preferred cruising altitude. Too low to have to worry about airline traffic, high enough to escape unwanted scrutiny. But just in case, he turned east, flew along for a minute or two, then turned south, flew some more, turned back west, then north again, his intended course.

At Loco Hills Elementary the children were waiting for him. His flyby's had attracted attention. Same thing at Wickett, Crane and Barnhart. Late that afternoon he landed at the small airport near Marfa, spotted the attendant and taxied over to him, following his instructions to park inside the low metal hangar. He shut his engine down, watched the hangar doors close behind him.

"Well, sir, you sure got things stirred up," the coverall-clad, grease-covered attendant shouted up at him. "Welcome to Marfa."

Halfway across Texas, just outside Austin, an FAA official called the local FBI office. "Someone in an old airplane seems to be putting on shows for school kids all across Texas. Even into New Mexico. The kids seem to know he's coming. They turn out and cheer."

The FBI agent seemed uncertain. "The kids in any danger? He coming in too close, too low?"

"From what we've been able to learn from a couple of school principals the pilot is careful," the FAA agent replied. "Doesn't fly right over the school, but probably violates minimum altitude requirements."

"So, what's the crime here?"

"I think someone stole the plane. A police officer in Roswell, New Mexico, said he had a close call. The guy hurried up when he saw the patrol car, headed right at him on the tarmac. Had to swerve to avoid that propeller chopping through his car. And him, I reckon."

The FBI agent perked up: "You say New Mexico? If he stole the plane, that might make this a federal crime. You know, crossing a state line. I'll look into this."

He was silent for a long moment, then: "But tell me: you say the kids at these schools know he's coming. How do they know that?"

"Beats me. But so far his shows have only played for one day. Maybe they were coincidences. Don't know where he is now. Maybe landed in a cow pasture somewhere and is hunkered down for the night. I'll let you know if he pops up again tomorrow."

"One more question," the FBI agent said. "I don't see any reports of a stolen airplane anywhere in the area. Not anywhere in the country. So, why do you think it's stolen?"

"Here's my best guess," FAA agent replied. "No flight plan has been filed and this is highly unusual behavior. It's an old airplane, a trainer of some sort, according to those who've seen it. The pilot paid cash for gas at Roswell. I'm thinking the owner of the plane doesn't yet know it's stolen. If I learn more, I'll let you know. Just consider this a head's up."

***

The old man was up early from the cot the Marfa attendant had set up for him, ate what was left of yesterday's sandwich and began tinkering with his airplane, walking all around it, checking, inspecting. "Three-sixty walkaround," he mused, remembering. Then wondered how he'd get the hangar door open, how he'd back the plane out onto the tarmac.

"Mornin', sir!" a friendly voice shouted from a still-greasy overall-clad attendant. The man was carrying two of Starbuck's best.

When the T-6 had been towed onto the tarmac and gassed up, and the old man was comfortably strapped in, the attendant climbed up onto the wing alongside the cockpit, smiled, and said, "The whole town will be following you today. How many shows you got planned?"

The old man scanned the wrinkled WAC chart on his lap, counted carefully, replied with a tired-sounding laugh, "Six in the morning, six in the afternoon. If...."

"If, what?"

"If they don't catch me."

By midmorning, the FAA agent was on the phone again with the FBI agent. "He's at it again. Buzzed three schools already. Very elusive. No one knows where he is now. I'm asking the Air National Guard to see if they can track him. But they won't be able to get into the air until tomorrow."

"Don't see any reports of a stolen plane yet," FBI replied.

"No, so he's holed up somewhere, probably getting fuel. I can't figure out where or how," FAA commented.

Halfway through his afternoon menu the old man saw a helicopter flying nearby, moving in alongside. He noticed it was painted gaudily, saw the words "KSAT-News 12" spelled out along the cabin. "Hah," he said, "TV. I better smile and wave." He did, then banked sharply away, pushed up the power, left the TV copter far behind.

The late afternoon crowds were bigger than before and the old man wasn't sure whether that was because the schools where he performed had more students, or whether local citizens were joining in. Either way, he was pleased.

That night he flew back to his safe haven in Marfa. The attendant was better dressed this time, took him in his car to the bar at the Hotel Paisano. The bar was packed and when he walked in with the airport attendant he was greeted with cheers. A man approached him, applauding, stuck out a hand.

"I'm the mayor. What you're doing is so great. Is that your own personal airplane?"

"No," the old man replied with a straight face. "I stole it."

Everyone laughed, everyone drank and as the old man

Alfred Kildow
Boothbay Harbor, ME

wobbled out to the attendant's car, he said: "Reminds me of the club at K2 in Korea. Drank a lot every night. Chased away the willies. Got up every morning after, early, flew two, sometimes three missions. Hard stuff. The heavy drinking seemed to help some. Took the edge off."

The crowds across Texas were huge that day and the old man, tired as he was from all that flying, was exhilarated. But he was also thankful it was his finale. He planned to turn himself in at day's end, back in Addison. Face the music.

FAA called FBI gleefully. "We got it," he shouted into the phone. "We'll get him today."

"What do you mean?" FBI asked. "How do we get him? And for what?"

FAA fairly giggled. "It's on Facebook. The whole schedule for today—except for midday when, if we haven't nailed him by then, he'll be getting gas."

"So how'd you figure that out?" FBI asked.

"Well, it helps to have a teen-aged daughter. She was all excited last night, talking about the airshow guy at dinner. Knew all about him. Knows who he is. Says all her friends are following him. Says he has more than a million 'likes,' whatever that is."

With two shows yet to go that afternoon, the old man wasn't particularly surprised when a pair of F-16 jet fighters pulled up and flanked him. He gave them a thumbs up, got one back. He could see the jets were staggering at his 200-knot cruising speed.

The pilot to his left gestured, pointing down. "They want me to land," the old man exclaimed to himself. He pointed to his own head, shook it side by side vigorously. The jet pilot pointed down again.

The old man throttled back, dropped a bit of flaps, slowed down to 90 knots. The jets peeled off. Way too slow for them. He watched them circle above him, then had a thought. He stretched down to the radio receiver and, sure

Alfred Kildow
Boothbay Harbor, ME

enough, there was a setting for the emergency channel, "Guard."

"Hey, F-16's, T-6 guy here, do you read?"

"Roger, T-6. They want you to land now."

"No way, 16. I got two shows left and the kids are waiting. You'll have to shoot me down to make me miss those shows."

"Roger, T-6. We know who you are and what you've been doing. If you land back at Addison like you say, you'll have an escort all the way. We'll be a bit above you, say at 20,000 feet or so. We'll track you on radar."

"Roger, 16. My show will go on just as scheduled. And I'll land at Addison right on my ETA. Seventeen hundred hours.

Roger, T-6. We'll try to keep you safe. You do the same."

The old man didn't bother to reply. He switched his radio to the Addison tower frequency and completed his scheduled shows, marveling at the dense crowds at both elementary schools. Felt good, battled a lump that began to form in his throat.

Five miles out from the Dallas-Fort Worth area half a dozen helicopters and several fixed-wing aircraft clustered about him. He ran a hand through his patchy gray hair. "I'm on the five o'clock news," he thought. A surprise. "Wonder what other surprises await me."

He called Addison tower and was cleared for immediate landing. Approaching the airport on downwind leg at 1,200 feet he was amazed to see vast crowds of people clogging the streets, bringing traffic to a standstill. He slid the canopy open, felt the rush of wind, wished he had goggles.

He turned base leg and radioed as though he was still in training, or landing at K2: "Addison. T-6 turning base, gear down and locked."

He heard a chuckle from the tower and a terse, "You're cleared to land."

A "follow me" jeep guided him toward the tarmac but had

Alfred Kildow
Boothbay Harbor, ME

to stop short. The crowd was beginning to push through a thin line of beleaguered Addison police. Two police officers climbed up onto the wing as he shut the engine off.

"You're under arrest, sir," one said. Then added: "I'm really sorry, sir. You're a hero. To me, anyway. And my kids. But I have my orders."

They climbed down together and the old man put his hands behind him for handcuffing.

"No way, sir. No cuffs from me."

They walked toward the crowded tarmac for a few paces and then the crowd burst through. He felt himself hoisted to the shoulders of two strong men and heard for the first time the cheers and shouts of the crowd.

He felt like Lindberg in Paris. But only for a brief moment. Then came the reckoning. He was carried through the crowd, then set down before a very officious looking trio: the chief of police, a man in a business suit and a familiar-looking, very serious face. He recognized him.

"You stole my airplane," the man said, his somber look beginning to crack.

The police chief cut in quickly: "The charge is theft of an airplane, taking it across state lines and using it for unlawful, unlicensed air shows."

The old man noticed for the first time the cameras and the microphones pointed his way.

Business suit spoke up, "I'm the attorney general here to formally charge you with these crimes. However...."

"However," the owner of the T-6 said softly, "I would have to sign the complaint. And I won't. On condition."

"And that might be?"

"You gotta let me see and touch your distinguished flying cross, the one you got after you flew your 150th mission and shot down your third Mig. Then you have to teach me that chandelle maneuver and show me how to fly this thing." He embraced the old man.

The cameras and microphones pushed closer.

Alfred Kildow
Boothbay Harbor, ME

"I can't do that," the old man replied. "I've made my last flight."

"And it was a doozy," the police chief said.

Soon it was all over. There was a press conference, flashing cameras, more cheering crowds. The chief himself drove him home in his old Chevy. His neighbors stood in their front yards, clapping.

He saw his 75-year-old neighbor standing on his lawn next door, wooden-faced. "I used to fly, you know," the old man said to his younger neighbor.

The man turned his back and walked inside without a word.

Alfred Kildow was a jet fighter pilot a very long time ago during the Korean War. He lives and writes in Boothbay Harbor, Maine. His novel "Fallout: remains of an atomic war," describes a mission he didn't fly, thankfully.

***

Steve Troyanovich
Florence, NJ

canto of the wind

y del silencio rozado apenas
por las alas de una lechuza

—Jorge Teillier

somewhere wings touch
the still hands of snow
listening for the return
of your vanishing warmth

S. Mason Pratt
Portland, ME

Skis on Snow

Ski boots crunch on new snow,
Icicles drip, form, and glisten.
Overhead, invisible jets write contrail lines up high
Across the cerulean blue sky.
And you listen,
And hear naught but the north wind
Blow through the evergreen trees.
It sighs and soughs,
Lifting white smoky puffs from snow laden boughs.
Sun pennies sparkle like lace,
Dazzling the eyes, warming the face.

Skis make new tracks, sound scratch, scratch,
Slicing through the white blanket o'er the land.
Poles thrust ahead, then pull back and push off,
In the powder so perfectly soft,
And kick, then swing a leg forward and glide.
Feel the sweat trickle down your back side.
Peel off layers, open collars, hear your heart pound,
Rest on your knees, in the sweet-scented pines not a
sound.
Ahead, a sight, my Standard Poodle, all black on white,
Still as a statue, her stare seems to say,
Come on now, we haven't all day!
The sun, no longer high in the western sky, now pink,
We stop, the cold water an elixir to drink.

And I think . . . deep in the woods, far from home,
Getting dark, a foreboding, alone.
Here in the wilderness
A cell phone is useless.

(continued)

S. Mason Pratt
Portland, ME

Back on the trail, she smells the bear scat,
And there are marks of the claws where it scratched.
Further on, scattered feathers, blood-red stains
Of a partridge, all that remains
From a sparrow hawk's talons and beak.
Our mood is now somber,
The day bright no longer.
You know, a Maine winter's not for the meek.

Off the trail, through maple and beech,
Using dead reckoning and by sheer force of will,
We finally reach the crest of the hill,
And there, to catch our breath, we stand
And cast our eyes upon the land,
And suddenly thrill
To see below the Christmas scene.
A wisp of smoke seen
From the farmhouse, lights
Cast their glow into the fast-approaching night.
Feel the welcome touch of snowflakes on your face,
And know she waits before a blazing fire.

And nothing more doth my heart desire
Than this, this time, this place,
Suffused with peacefulness and grace.
Then downhill slide and glide,
Dog bounding behind,
And I suddenly find
The snow's too deep, I've schussed too fast.
Tumbling in powder, arms and legs akimbo, alas,
Embedded and stuck in my bindings.
So release them, get off them, and I feel
A wet tongue on my face.
So it's haste
In my struggle to get up into the air.

(continued)

S. Mason Pratt
Portland, ME

There's snow down my neck and all over my hair,
And we're happy to hoof it with skis over shoulder.
Now nothing can hold her.
She races ahead, I yell, "Let's go!"
And I know
That soon we'll be warming our paws and our toes,
So we romp through the mantel of fresh fallen snow.

***

Sally Belenardo
Branford, CT

Earthworm

It would be wrong
to think the earthworm,
unsung tenant of the soil,
when eaten by the Robin,
dies, forever gone,

for its flesh becomes
the energy expended
as the Robin flies,
and the silence of its life
becomes a song.

Judy O'Dell
Rockport, ME

Ambrose the Special Seagull

First day of spring. I am standing at the town dock in Blue Hill, Maine. Mill Stream empties into the bay over a small dam, and ducks and gulls are swimming in the moving water. A flock of ring-billed gulls lands on the paved parking area. A juvenile wearing its camouflage feathers strolls up and down the boat ramp. Several adults keep watch from the tops of the pilings. I walk among them. A few rise up, flap their wings and land in another spot. I wonder if these are relatives of Ambrose, the Special Seagull.

June 1981. We are on vacation in Ocean City, NJ. My three sons are happy that their beloved grandparents are with us. On our first day at the beach, Tom, the three-year-old, waves half of a peanut butter and jelly sandwich above his head. A gull swoops down and grabs it. He begins to cry, partly from surprise and partly from rage, that the gull stole his sandwich. My father-in-law is sitting next to him and pulls him onto his lap.

"Tom, it's okay. That was Ambrose, a very special seagull. He is famous around here."

Tom stops crying and looks at his grandfather.

Albert, the skeptical seven-year-old, remarks, "Pop-Pop, you are making that up. All of these birds look the same."

"Oh no," his grandfather replies. "If you had looked closely, you would have noticed that Ambrose was different from the other gulls flying around here."

"Why," asks four-year-old Paul, using his favorite word.

"Ambrose is a ring-billed gull. He has a black ring around his beak, yellow legs, and his wings have black on the tips with white spots. Those flying overhead now have pinkish legs and white heads. They are herring gulls. The ones with black heads are laughing gulls."

Albert stands up and looks at the gulls circling overhead.

Judy O'Dell
Rockport, ME

"How do you know his name is Ambrose?"

His grandfather pauses for a moment to come up with an answer. The three boys look at him.

"Well, I was walking the beach early this morning, and a ring-billed gull was standing alone by the water. I said hello, and he told me his name was Ambrose. He had just arrived from Florida where he spent the winter."

"Seagulls don't talk, Pop-Pop," Albert says.

"Oh, but Ambrose does. That's why he is a special seagull." Albert is not sure whether to believe him.

Tom climbs out of his grandfather's lap and resumes eating the other half of his sandwich. I stand by to make sure there is not another gull attack. I don't notice that Paul has left his Doritos on a paper plate on the other blanket. Whoosh, Ambrose is back and snags a Dorito.

"He's back," Albert says excitedly. "I saw his yellow legs."

I pack up the picnic lunch.

That evening after dinner, the boys want to go back to the beach to look for Ambrose. The gulls circle overhead as we walk to the edge of the ocean. I throw some crackers in the air. The boys clap when the gulls catch them. We see only one gull with yellow legs, and the boys shout hello to Ambrose.

After the boys are in bed, I ask my father-in-law how he knows so much about gulls. He tells me that he was stationed at the airbase at Horsham—St Faith during the war, about 40 miles from the English Channel. He studied the sea birds around the base to kill time between missions. All I knew of his war service was that he was in the Army Air Corps. He tells me he was an armorer-gunner on B-24 Liberators. That is all he would say.

For the rest of the week, Ambrose is a presence at lunchtime. The boys feed him bread crusts and Doritos. We look for him in the evenings on the beach. My father-in-law's Ambrose bedtime stories become more elaborate. Ambrose is the largest and strongest gull on the beach. He has a mate called Angela. We haven't seen her because she is sitting on her nest near the bay. Ambrose goes out searching for food, flying up and down the shore looking for her favorite fish. He fights off a fox that wants to steal her eggs. He grabs a snake crawling near the nest, flies out over the ocean, and drops it. He spies a clam, dips down to pick it up, flies up, and lets it smash on the boardwalk to break the shell, then dives down for his meal. When it gets too cold in New Jersey, Ambrose and Angela fly south. They can drink saltwater on their long flights if they get thirsty. One year they flew to Cuba, and another year they went to Mexico. Disney World in Orlando is their favorite winter place. They stop to eat near fast-food restaurants where there are open trash containers. Ambrose loves French fries. They fly over fishing boats hoping to steal the bait. They fly over farm fields, landing to eat mice and insects. Ambrose sometimes gets in fights with herring gulls when they try to steal his food. He always wins. The stories end with "every summer Ambrose flies back to Ocean City to see Al, Paul, and Tom."

That was my father-in-law's last summer. He died the following June from cancer, probably caused by the chemicals he used in the dry cleaning and formal wear business he started after the war. A few years later, we found a photo on the wall at the Smithsonian Air and Space Museum of someone who looked like him posed with a crew in front of a B24 Liberator named "A Dog's Life" with flack holes visible in its side.

My mother-in-law's sight faded. When she was preparing to move from the house that was her home for fifty years, she asked my sons to go through some boxes and tell her what was in them. One of them contained their grandfather's war diary and photographs of him, his crewmates, and some of the B24's they flew. They discovered that he was a 24-year-old sergeant with the 755 Squadron, 458th Bombardment Group, Army Air Corps, that participated in the decisive air campaigns after D-Day. He flew over France, the

Judy O'Dell
Rockport, ME

Netherlands, Belgium, and Germany. The diary entries confirmed that it was him in the photo at the museum and described harrowing details of 27 missions. Among his awards were a Distinguished Flying Medal and a Silver Star.

But his grandsons remember him for the legend of Ambrose the Special Seagull that lives on in the stories they tell their children when sitting on the beach in Ocean City.

***

Bill Herring
Minnetonka, MN

Numbers

for Sean, age 4

With my fingers
I can count to ten.

With my toes
I can count to twenty.

With my imagination
I can count the stars
in the universe.

J. A. Pollard
Winslow, ME

Bears

Children are the saviors of mankind
Not creeds
Not epithets
Not long harangues
in public squares
Nor incensed prayers

But children
helpless in their innocence
delightful in their ignorance
Still unafraid of—Bears!

***

Joanne McNamara
Wells, ME

Walter

Windowpanes look out to the ocean, yet inside, reflect
        uncertainty, confusion, and sadness.
After the rain, steam rises from the ground, encasing the
        cottage in smoke.
Love of a life gone by drifts in and out of his mind;
        memories pique his interest and then fade.
There are few visitors, only sweet vignettes of coherent time
        with her.
Even keeled is an unknown quality to this man.
Reaping the seeds of a lifetime, he sits waiting for his
        demise.

Cindy Partington
Dallas Center, IA

Riches

there was always lots of laughter
and kindness
but I knew we were poor
baskets of hand me downs from
a neighbor or cousin
a great delight to try on and share
with sisters, but never quite the right size
no second helpings
popcorn for a treat
no summer camps
never a family vacation
no newspaper subscription
fixer upper bikes, one left in the alley
and the garbage man took it away
one toy for Christmas
while seeing piles of wrapped boxes
elsewhere

no eating out—I remember the one time
step-grandpa's treat
free entertainment, penny ante poker for adults,
jacks, cops & robbers, snow ball fights,
swings, a slide, a jungle gym at the park

no heat in our attic dorm
well-frayed and faded blankets
on icy nights we three girls slept in one bed
to keep warm, while baby brother slept downstairs

Cindy Partington
Dallas Center, IA

Mom believed we were rich
beyond her dreams
they were buying a house!
no sleeping in a car
no living with relatives apart from her family
no one pair of good shoes to share with sisters
extra food in a cupboard
milk delivered three times a week
a used wringer washer, a clothesline, a backyard
a Christmas toy for each of her four children
heat on the main floor
church choirs for her children to sing in

Mom was oh so right
we had no hot dogs, no bologna,
no Wonder Bread, no chips or pop, no Oleo
because she wanted us to eat healthy food
because there was no extra cash
we all learned to clean, to repair,
to do chores of all kinds,
inside and out, learned the value of work,
skills for living
we played outside year round
in safety
we walked to school and it felt good
we were given the gift of
"do the right thing" to live by
with the addition of
"you'll know in your heart what that is"

all four of us marvel at how lucky and rich
and blessed we were

E. M. Barsalou
Dover, NH

Seductive Sky

The sky was on fire, truly beautiful and seductive,
entrancing me with her novel authority; the reds, the blues.
It grew above all clouding over a mirrored lake that
Surely has advanced over a mountain view that didn't
Go away, climbing high in the sky to only revert back to the
tide.
Blacker than black when ice would melt away,
Translucent and depraved; glowing off an illuminance
Of your soul-posturing just like this day.
No wind, no song birds, no children playing; no such
Wildlife roaming, distant, conquering—Oh the admission.
Ponder onto greater things of how it might have been.
Deciding it was either now or then, but as I had been taken
Back by greater things, I rest my mind to many thoughts
I'd had when I could hold my breath and just relax.

***

Patrick T. Randolph
Lincoln, NE

February

Distant whistle of the train—
Snow falls—
small flakes, as fragile as morning thoughts,
flicker carefully

Against the living room windowpane
Until a poem gathers on the glass.

Dorothy M. Weiss
Orlando, FL

Far Away Places and Strange Sounding Names

Inspired by the Bing Crosby record, "Far Away Places with Strange Sounding Names," and those comedy adventure "On the Road" movies starring Bob Hope and Dorothy Lamour, "Mutiny on the Bounty," the Marlon Brando film version—I longed for Tahiti, French Polynesia and the islands in the South Pacific Ocean.

I worked for Pan American Airways, so we flew there on "my" airline spending a three week vacation in my dream destination, Tahiti and its outer islands, Moorea and Bora Bora. Without my employee discount on air costs and hotel rooms, it would not have been possible to realize my dream. My husband and I were thrilled.

Lush green foliage dotting tropical shorelines, soft warm sea breezes, white sandy powdered sugar-like beaches, perfumed hibiscus flowers of every color everywhere, welcomed us as we settled into our thatched roof bungalow. We could look down through the glasslike, transparent floor at the turquoise water and see little fishes swimming below.

One day on one of our excursions—a boat trip to Moorea —I chose to stay above deck, actually leaning against the front bow of the boat in my gift-shop sarong with hibiscus flowers in my hair as I had seen Dorothy Lamour do in those films singing her songs.

"Come inside," the captain warned, "you're going to get soaked when we increase speed.

"No," I laughed. "I want to do this. I have dreamed of this for years."

My husband said, "Let her do it."

The captain looked at me, smiled and winked, "Okay, here we go!"

It was an exhilarating ride. I got drenched, soaked to the

Dorothy M. Weiss
Orlando, FL

skin. I didn't care. I loved every moment. I looked like a drowned rat. I didn't look like Dorothy Lamour but I was happy. They wrapped me in towels when the boat docked. "Thank you," I murmured to the captain.

"You're welcome," he grinned. "Every now and then, I channel Johnny Weissmuller, as I dive off the cliffs and swim in the lagoon like he did in those Tarzan movies."

So I got to live my dream. Even put on a grass skirt and danced and swayed with laughing Tahitiens encouraging me to come and dance with them on our last night there at a farewell party given for all guests at our hotel. Pan Am is gone. The Pan American World Airways that I worked for—loved and received a worldwide education in travel and tourism—no longer exists. My beloved husband is also gone. He passed away last year. I treasure Tahiti and the fun, fantasy moments there. Golden memories. Thank you Bing Crosby, Bob Hope, Dorothy Lamour, and Marlon Brando. I wonder who else you inspired to travel and dare to fulfill their dreams of fun and adventure?

***

Steve Troyanovich
Florence, NJ

obituary

In oblivion he made a life

—Najwan Darwish

... he came
 he saw
 he left...

Neil Cote
Saco, ME

Lupine Lady

Like lupines on the hillside, she's wild and she's free,
Free for all the taking and pretty as can be.
When the rains of April wet the grounds for spring
Soon she will be rambling north and what joy she brings.
Clad in many colors she favors purple most,
White, pink, rouge and yellow, other hues she boasts.
Kittery to Caribou she's waving in the breeze
Soaking up the sunlight, giving you the tease.
Caught up with her in Yarmouth, only not for long
Those Midcoast hills were calling her and she heard their song
But just around to turn some heads and then was on her way
Bar Harbor, Calais, Eastport, up past Frenchman Bay.
You've heard the Lupine Lady and how she scattered seeds
Like Johnny Appleseed, wondrous was her deed.
The early hue of summer bears her loving hand
Just beyond the solstice, is she ever grand.
But don't try to hold her, she's just a passing fling
Disappears before July like monarch on the wing.
Takes back her colors early but you needn't shed a tear
Maine's blessed by Lupine Lady, she'll be back next year.

San D. Hasselman
Boothbay Harbor, ME

Independence River

Under the purple warp
of eve's sky
we glide
through reflections
of errant trees.

Our tandem hands and hearts
dig circles,
we glide
pulling canoe
and marriage too.

Swallows swoop up insects
silently,
we glide
lifting paddles
dripping tannin.

Rushing waters signal
frayed edges,
we glide
our watchful eyes
search for meaning and clues.

Flat paddles now defend
no longer
gliding
shielding this bow
and life alike.

San D. Hasselman
Boothbay Harbor, ME

Haystacks abounding
exposing
ripping
the waters apart
crushing spirit.

Quickly the river leaps
pouncing and
marking
my ample lap
with nature's sweat.

From the back he guides her
flicking his
strong wrists
aiming our lives
and canoe too.

Arrowed, we head for calm
through shoots of
walled
water frothed with
white laced edges.

Margie Thumm
Raymond, ME

My April Fool Jewel

I got the call
Tomorrow, April First, was the day
When in my arms she would lay.
A cute wee girl
Her hair so brown,
Soft as down.
Her wary look at me,
Who is she?
Little then did I know,
How I would walk,
She would run
Through the coming years.
There were challenges and tears.
Smart, pretty, determined.
Tenacious to be exact.
A capable and loving woman, now.
Still determined, tenacious in fact.
Her adoption was no April Fool.
She is my shining April Jewel.

Mimi Edmunds
Rockport, ME

Debris

Every summer, wherever I was living and wherever I was working, I would come to Rockport, Maine, to teach documentary filmmaking at Maine Media, a school of photography and film workshops dedicated to the art of visual storytelling. My ten-year-old daughter got to come along with me every year since she was born.

The summer of 2002 has a special memory with the arrival of an unusual student, Captain David McDowell Brown, United States Navy, astronaut, mission specialist, selected to fly with the Columbia Space Shuttle later that summer. At 46, he fit the physical profile of a pilot in the space program; over six feet, with a full muscular build, square face, blue eyes and freckles, sandy red-brown hair and a wide, ready smile. Your humble American astronaut.

Dave Brown had come to The Workshops to take a course using the small home video camera to document and tell a story. He enrolled in a camera class with a noted documentary filmmaker. The small cameras were becoming a popular trend as their mobility made filmmaking accessible to anyone. At the same time I was teaching a workshop on how to produce a feature interview for a documentary. The classes were working side by side. My students saw Dave's presence as an exciting and rare opportunity to try out their interviewing techniques. This was an ideal practice situation for the real world of an aspiring journalist. The Workshops provide a protective cocoon, simulating actual experiences, and allowing students to learn by experimenting, taking risks and making mistakes, all in a safe environment.

Dave Brown was not only modest, he was concerned that the inevitable attention his presence might draw would interrupt the work going on in other classes, so he requested to be kept at a low profile. However, when my students asked

Mimi Edmunds
Rockport, ME

him if he would agree to be interviewed for their class project, he warmly responded that he'd be glad to talk with them, as long as it was discreet and didn't interfere with what else was happening on campus.

At first Captain Brown seemed reticent to talk about the details of his work, maybe it was the reticence of humility or shyness, but after a short time it was clear he was profoundly excited with the experimental research he was assigned as mission specialist for this shuttle flight. The curiosity of my students opened a treasure door of questions: How did he become an astronaut? What was the mission of this flight? What was he looking forward to in his role? And of course, how in the world did he end up here in little Rockport, Maine, just before he was to fly?

Once given the green light to prepare for the interview, the students set about cramming to gather research and background on Captain Brown, the space program, and the Columbia shuttle in order to draft a competent interview. They had little time. Workshops only lasted a week and they would have to film and edit in less than three days. After establishing a time and place, they invited Dave to sit outside behind the classrooms on a bench under a tree while they gathered around him on the grass to ask their questions. A student from Ohio opened the interview.

"Captain Brown, we understand you're an astronaut on the upcoming Columbia shuttle."

Dave nodded shyly, and started to smile, but kept a serious posture.

"What brought you up here to Rockport Maine, to take a workshop at this time? Shouldn't you be preparing for the launch?"

Looking around at each student, Dave had them on the edge of their seats as he responded in a quiet deadpan tone.

"Well," pausing, with the hint of a smile, "My flight was cancelled."

The students looked at each other, and then openly

laughed, immediately at ease. Dave went on to explain that NASA had to delay the shuttle launch for several months to repair faulty tiles. A haunting reminder of the Challenger shuttle disaster sixteen years earlier lingered in his words. I remembered and shivered. The students went on.

"Have you ever flown on a shuttle before, Captain Brown?"

"No, no, this is my first. And it's going to be an exciting one because we have a unique crew—there are seven of us, including two women, one of whom is from India, a Russian, an Israeli, a Palestinian, and an African American. It's also a special flight because it's going to be heavily geared toward research, looking at a host of issues useful for space and for science. We all have different specialties and each of us has certain specific jobs."

Dave went on to say that he had followed the Apollo and Gemini space flights as a kid, "I thought this was the coolest job you could ever have, but I never saw this path for myself."

"You have no fears about flying in space?"

"No, not really. In fact, the most frightening experience in this business I've ever had was not in space. It was landing the biggest fighter jet on an aircraft carrier, in the middle of the ocean, in the middle of the night. *That* was scary. It has to be perfect, there's no room for error."

"You're not afraid, at all?" persisted one student.

Dave leaned back, and in a serious tone answered with assurance.

"No, I'm not at all afraid. This is so organized, researched, and secure. We go through a training of simulated malfunctions where our job is to deal with the problem. Once you get through these trials you're ready."

"Why is it necessary to send people?'

"I think because people can come back and talk about it, I guess that's storytelling."

"And you're here now. What do you hope to learn in your workshop?"

Mimi Edmunds
Rockport, ME

Suddenly Dave became very animated. It was as if this was the first question that excited him, the one he really had been waiting to answer.

"I want to make a personal video on this flight, showing a group of people at work...sort of like at a backyard barbecue. It will be a video for students at all levels, telling the story of flying the shuttle from inside, showing them what it's like to fly in space, recorded with a small video camera. It will be as if they were there, as if all of *you* were with us in the shuttle."

He continued to answer questions and tell stories for the next couple of hours as a navy pilot preparing for a space flight.

***

That afternoon I brought my daughter, Eliza, onto the campus. She knew little about the space program but was always inquisitive when she met someone who did something so different from her world. She had been profoundly affected by 9/11 the year before, knowing that two of her cousins were in New York City at the time. She was conscious of a larger world, but it was a world she regarded with a certain amount of awe and fear. I wanted her to meet Dave Brown. When he introduced himself as an astronaut preparing for a space flight, she shyly looked up at his six-foot-two frame from four-foot-eight, enrapt.

He stooped down to her and asked, "Eliza, what would you like me to bring you from space?"

"Hmmm...hmm, let me think..." was all she could manage to get out.

I was anxious for her to answer and say something, but whenever she was asked a big question requiring serious thought or a decision, she would deliberate with, "I'm thinking...hmmm, I'm still thinking."

So, Dave decided to make a gentle suggestion. "Well, I

think I have an idea, I'm going to bring you a beautiful picture of the earth taken from space. Just for you."

Then Eliza posed a statement-question that they both understood only in the way these two beings from such polar opposite perspectives could, at this time in their lives, she said, "Showing how big we are, how small we are?"

***

Six months later, the Columbia Space Shuttle was rescheduled to launch on January 16th. A month before the launch, Dave sent an email to members of his workshop telling them how much his time at The Workshops had meant to him, thanking them for all he had learned and promising he was going to put it to good use on the shuttle trip.

The launch went forward. Living in Tucson at the time Eliza and I watched the takeoff, excited that we knew somebody inside that shuttle on his way to space. We pulled up a picture of Dave and Eliza sitting on the lawn at the Workshops six months earlier. Then we went back to our everyday lives and let the shuttle flight and Captain Dave Brown recede to the back burner for the time being. On the night before the Columbia was to re-enter the earth's orbit on its return, Dave Brown sent a message to NASA in which he said that, while space was exciting, nothing was more beautiful than the earth, or being a part of it.

***

On Saturday morning, February 1, 2003, we woke up early anticipating the return of the Columbia, only to hear that the shuttle was "lost." Lost? How could it be lost? Shortly thereafter, we heard that it was entering the atmosphere in "pieces"—breaking apart—and disintegrating over the American southwest and that debris was falling every-

Mimi Edmunds
Rockport, ME

where. For days and days following, all the news repeated many times over was this concept of "debris." Eliza and I were frozen, unable to talk. We just hugged each other, and hoped it wasn't really true, that Dave would come back. The next day we both let our pens fly.

Debris

Floating, flying, slamming, roaming,
sailing, crashing, driving, diving,
turning, twisting, swirling.
Tell us where you are. You are not debris, no Dave you are
not, you are...
Was it debris that caused you to fall?
Was it debris that made your children, your parents, your
friends, call out your Name?
Debris was the Word of the Day.
Today it means disintegration, destruction, disappearance,
reflecting back on us—
"Showing us how small we are, how big we are."
Debris is what is left behind in the wake.
Your wake, no. We are left in your wake.
We feel the debris in the air
in our hearts, in what our heads cannot see.
We feel your presence Dave and we do not understand
the truth of your disappearance.

Mimi Edmunds
Rockport, ME

Can you not climb back in and put together your house,
removing that debris?
Or is that debris the broken pieces of your heart, our hearts,
when we hear that you're not coming back, none of you.
That you will not be returning with a little girl's request,
Your promise, a photograph of the earth—from space.
Made just by you—in space—for her. Special.
Perhaps the last piece of debris could be
a picture floating down through the atmosphere—over
Tucson maybe—
the atmosphere that inhaled you, perhaps that little piece of
debris
could become a shard of beauty and light
for a ten-year-old girl waiting for you
to keep your promise.

Let it float,
Let it be weightless,
Like you in space—
Let it bring you back,
so that the debris is actually
that indomitable spirit of curiosity
to know the universe that holds our earth in its sphere—
Captured in a traveling photograph
of a luminescent globe floating
in a kaleidoscopic sea of indigo.
Letting us know—
you are not debris.
You are intact and we will not become
the debris in your wake.
Why couldn't you have come back?
Instead of that "debris" they keep talking about,
She asks. Let that debris come to life and soar again
Let it be, let it be—

Mimi Edmunds
Rockport, ME

Dear Diary,

Tradgety struk again. A NASA ship exploded. Around 9:15 Eastern. 15 minutes before it was going to land.

One of the astronots was our friend, Dave Brown! I'm going to fast for a day because I'm so depressed.

He told me last summer when he was a student, "Don't forget that I'm going to give you a picture of the earth." Those were the last words heard from him. We will never see him again.

All day I was hoping they survived. I've been feeling sick all day long. But now I know I won't be seeing him ever or at least till I die.

We met him at my mom's workshop in Maine. He just wanted to help kids learn about Space.

Right now I feel like I'm going to throw up.

Love,

Eliza

***

Patrick T. Randolph
Lincoln, NE

Sweeping the Sky

Bare tree branches jutting upwards—
Slender black silhouettes—
These Winter brooms
Work with the morning winds,
Sweeping away the clouds—
Leaving a bright clear brilliant blue.

One bird finds her voice—
And carries it cautiously across the Sky
Like the young mother holding a small child in her arms.

Darrell McBreairty
Allagash, ME

Allagash

An echo of a memory
is all that will remain
in the recesses of the forest
for someone to reclaim
when the dust of our lives
has disappeared
and been forgotten
by those who once loved us
and they too have passed on.

Nothing but empty
and the shadow of evening
drifting over the remnants
of our stones
will suggest
that this was once a village
peopled with voices
now silent and gone.

The sound of a pole pick
on the stones of the river
as the last river driver
disappears in the dusk
will haunt the hollows
and fade into the hills
as night descends
and we are no more.

Genie Dailey
Jefferson, ME

Triumvirate

Court is now in session.
I wake to the raucous cacophony
of three crows who visit daily.
They perch in the uppermost
branches of a big bare maple that
hovers over my wintry yard.

No doubt they're discussing—
in no uncertain terms—
the poor state of affairs
at my bird feeders.
Squawking, buzzing, and chattering,
they present their prosecutorial opinion
on my dereliction of duty.

It's not as if they can actually *use*
the feeders I have out there;
these three black beauties
are much too big and heavy
to cling to the slender perches.
Instead, they strut their stuff
on the snow below when it's dappled
with seeds dropped by others.

They're not embarrassed in the least
about helping themselves to the leftovers.
These crows are proud and self-assured
(as any good prosecutor should be),
and I know they are handing down
a guilty verdict this morning.

Time to get dressed and take care of
those empty bird feeders...
and apologize to the Triumvirate.

Kaye Nelson Ratliff
Wadesboro, NC

Goth

A curtain of black-tinted hair
falls across half of the beautiful face
of the girl who sits on my office couch.
The eye I can see is ebony lined

and the lips as dark as old blood.
Half-gloves cover the wrists and arms
where the blade has let out the tortured life
concealed inside her veins.

Her brow, nose and tongue are sharply pierced,
impaled by tiny lances, mirroring the ravaging of her soul,
and the beginnings of her woman softness are hidden
beneath the bleak black weight of her clothes.

Her whole dark appearance screams look, but don't see me,
don't see the shattering soul within.
Look, but don't see me,
don't see the pain my body can't contain.

And so, in this place where black-clad angels
come to do Armageddon battle with their demons
I don my armor and make the first sally
and ask, "What brings you here today?"

Alice Mello
Bucksport, ME

Ocean's Edge

Perched upon the tree,
that was drawn out to the ocean by the blazing sunlight.
The same sun that allows the diamonds to dance atop the
ocean waves.

We sit, we stare, we dream of moments past and those yet
to come.
Tip-toeing along the rocky shore,
leaping from rock-to-rock, attempting to stay above the
mud-drenched flat.

Waves crashing,

The voice of the gulls as they speak to one another,
mating calls one could assume.
Diving, splashing into the water—to grasp a fish,
then back on to a nearby rock,
fighting to keep its prize from the many other gulls—
jealous of his speckled catch.
The wind blowing, rustling the tall grass that lines the
inner shore.
Healing, therapeutic to the inner depths of the soul.
A visit to the ocean on any given day—today, tomorrow,
or even a visit from yesterday.

John T. Hagan
Springboro, OH

A Sports Reflection

Make no mistake, I have always loved to play sports and watch sporting events, whether they be team or individual competitions. Unfortunately, I never enjoyed enough size or skill to play organized football, basketball, or baseball above the junior high, Catholic Youth Organization level. My huge all-male high school of nearly 1,700 students was far too rich in talent and brawn to allow for my participation. My two sons, however, were each able to play football and baseball for four years for a very competitive Catholic high school. The younger of the two continued his football experience at the collegiate, Division-III level.

My zealous interest in sports, however, has over the years been eroded or sobered by the hype, commercialization, and prima donnas attendant to nearly every level of the fields or surfaces of play.

The genesis of my passion for sports began at age four when I accompanied my father to my oldest brother's freshman high school basketball games for the same all-male school my other older brother and I would eventually attend. While my oldest brother would go on to play four years of high school football and basketball, making all-area teams in both, and four years of varsity football at West Point, it was his freshman high school basketball season that provided my defining observation.

Sitting next to my father, who was himself a high school baseball, basketball, and football player, and a college baseball player, I probably drifted in and out of attention to each game, much like a four-year-old would. (My mother rarely attended, as she hated sports.) I was, however, conscious enough of the action and my dad's exhortations to develop an astute understanding of the rudiments of the game. I don't recall exactly in what circumstance, I was first asked,

John T. Hagan
Springboro, OH

"Johnny, how do you play basketball?" In my cut-to-the-chase, Occam's Razor response, I'm told I replied in my four-year-old's parlance, "Ya bounce it and ya bounce it, and ya frow it inna bakset." Apparently finding my succinct characterization of this often nail-biting competition quaint, I was for a few months at least asked to repeat my in-depth analysis of the dynamics of basketball.

Making every effort to re-create the action of basketball games in the living room of our very small bungalow home, I would for a number of months use the archway between our living room and dining room to shoot my miniature basketball against, often repeating, "Ya bounce it and ya bounce it, and ya frow it inna bakset." As often as not, of course, I would miss the archway and launch the ball over the dining room table and topple my long-suffering mother's few remaining delicate, buffet items that had escaped the carnage of three rambunctious boys in a two-bedroom, one bathroom (tub, no shower), living room, dining room, and kitchen home.

Over the years I have watched with dismay the ever-escalating hype and commercialization of college football and basketball that is now cascading on to the ranks of high school competition: to wit, the National Kickoff Classic and the Flyin' to the Hoops extravaganzas. What is particularly offensive to me is the chest beating egotism of football, basketball, and baseball players at the collegiate but more conspicuously at the professional level. The pros are often compensated with obscenely exorbitant salaries and rendered the homage of demigods while those in the real world provide critical human services for which they are paid minimally and given short shrift. Many years ago, I read in a sports publication the observation of a National Basketball Association player of no less stature than the legendary Bob Cousy. Recalling as best I can, this floor wizard was amazed that people would pay enormous sums to professional basketball players to play what he called "a child's game." What

John T. Hagan
Springboro, OH

is notable here are two factors: first, the salaries of professional basketball players of Cousy's era would be pocket change for our current luminaries, and second, his pithy characterization of lofty and dazzling professional basketball as "a child's game" might evoke, "Let him be anathema!"

When I consider the current practice of some professional athletes pontificating upon social issues on the strength of their assumed mastery of the complexities of human history and interaction, I am curious as to how making three-point shots and three-sixty slam dunks imbues them with such profundity. When I watch professional athletes refusing to show respect for a flag that represents the gallant efforts of those who endured incalculable suffering on battlegrounds of frozen turf and insect infested heat, those who today are without limbs or pain-free lives, those who are buried in graves or lying decomposed throughout the Pacific and European theatres, those who shivered and nearly starved before the Battle of Trenton, or those who froze in foxholes in the Ardennes awaiting the next round of German 88's to blast themselves like their comrades to pieces into tree limbs; I am appalled by the contempt shown for a nation that affords these preening peacocks a standard of living that ranks with the lifestyles and comforts of the monarchs and oligarchs of the world.

To those professional athletes who use Twitter and Facebook and other social media to rail against "systemic American flaws," (and you know who you are) to talk down to us grunts who rear our children, pay our bills, respect the rule of law, and revere the sacrifices of those who provided and protected our many freedoms; I suggest you reconsider just how critical your "child's game" is to the total human condition. Reduced to its essence, "Ya bounce it, and ya bounce it, and ya frow it inna bakset."

Irene Zimmerman
Greenfield, WI

Staying at Your Summer Home Without You

for D.D.

Leaving Old Beach Road, I drive down the narrow
lane between stately hardwoods and pull up
at the front door. In the window flower boxes,
pansies belie the fact that this, your summer home,
has been vacant since last year. I find the key
where your gardener placed it and let myself in.

Your husband's walker stands in the entranceway.
The piano is open, a Mozart sonata waiting
to be played. Folding chairs are neatly stacked
near glass doors that reveal the deck overlooking
the bay. I carry in laptop and clothes from the car,
grab a book of poems and move outside.

At the feeders below, sparrows squabble with a squirrel.
A path of woodchips, bordered by mums and sedum,
leads to a grassy expanse that slopes down to the pier.
I want you to feel at home, you said last night
on the phone. *Knowing you're there, in my paradise,*
is next best to being there myself.

Last year we spent afternoons out here, writing
poems for the workshop, talking only rarely for help
to find a word or check the rhythm of a line.
We've stopped writing emails. *My fingers burn*
from the chemo, you told me. *It hurts just to touch*
the keys. I open my book and try to settle in.

Irene Zimmerman
Greenfield, WI

The sun is cutting diamonds on the water. A gust of wind
riffles the pages. Chilly, I go inside for a sweater
and decide to stay. Here in the living room, everything
speaks of you—a watercolor done by a local artist,
books of poetry stacked on a side table, your
granddaughters
smiling from a silver frame on the window ledge.

Everything here is waiting for you to come home.

***

Steve Troyanovich
Florence, NJ

forever blue

... estas dentro de mi sangre
y pasas por mi corazon a cada rato.
—Juan Rolfo

between childhood slumber
and aging sorrows
final whispers fade
into faltering blue

Julie Babb
Damariscotta, ME

Today

Today I went down to the sea
Because I could.
Because I can
Still feel the pebbles beneath my feet;
Hear the song sparrow's highest notes
Above the ocean's thrust;
Watch the newly-minted Eider pair
Ride as one on the incoming swells.

Today I went down to the sea
Because I could.
Because I can
Still breathe winter's leftover chill;
Watch the angel wings of the gulls
As they swirl against the sky;
Scatter last year's golden seeds
Into the green and growing spring.

Today I went down to the sea
Because I could,
Because I still can.

David S. Holt
Jacksonville, FL

A Romantic Question?

We bought our tickets months in advance for the *Jersey Boys,* the Broadway show that profiles the rise of the 1960's singing group, The Four Seasons. I loved the music from the '60's, and Carole liked much of the popular music from that period also. As we read the previews of the show we became more enthused with the prospect of reliving our younger years through our musical memories.

The lead singer, Franke Valli, released two songs that topped the charts, "My Eyes Adored You" and "Can't Take My Eyes Off You." Those songs typified the way Carole and I looked at each other in our early years as our relationship was blossoming. Much of our relationship developed around dates that included dining, conversing and gazing across the table at each other with eyes of love.

We decided that dinner at Larkin's on the River in Greenville, SC before the show at the neighboring Peace Center for the Performing Arts would add a nice romantic touch. I made the reservations for five o'clock so we would have plenty of time to enjoy the ambiance beside the Reedy River and wine with our meal before the curtain opened at 7:30 P.M.

Arriving at Larkin's, a dilemma faced us when the hostess asked where we would like to dine. Carole loves dining al fresco, and the canopied tables beside the building and close to the river sang their siren song. However, heat, humidity, and possible showers pushed us into the cool, dry interior and a circular booth where we could sit next to each other.

The sparkling bubbles in our champagne flutes almost matched the sparkle in Carole's eyes as we toasted our good fortune at finding each other. One bowl of she-crab soup was served with two spoons as we requested, and the chef split one spinach salad onto two plates for our second

David S. Holt
Jacksonville, FL

course. We savored our entrees, our time together and tried to ignore the lightning flashes and then the downpour.

All we had was an umbrella that was barely three feet across, and it wouldn't give much protection—even for one person. As we dithered about how to stay dry over the two hundred feet between Larkin's and the closest entrance to the Peace Center, the rain abated.

Dashing up the stairs without using the umbrella, the lighter rain barely dampened our clothes, but Carole's sandals provided no protection for her toes. Inside the Peace Center Carole bemoaned her wet feet, but I told her we'd soon think of our run in the rain as part of our romantic evening. We found our seats in the lower balcony, settled in and began looking at the program.

Upon getting the reminder to turn off all cell phones, Carole took hers out of her purse and went through the complete shut-down process while I watched others around us doing the same.

During the first half of the program we heard, "Sherry," the first big hit by The Four Seasons, and others came in quick succession. When Frankie sang, "My Eyes Adored You," we looked at each other, intertwined fingers and squeezed.

The storyline was important, but I was there for the music, and when Frankie began singing, "Can't Take My Eyes Off You" the audience erupted in applause. I just looked at Carole, and she returned my loving gaze.

At the end of our romantic performance, as the applause died down and the lights came up, Carole leaned over and asked, "Darling, will you turn me on?"

Whoa! I haven't had an invitation like that in a long time.

Then she handed me her cell phone.

Lucia Owen
Stoneham, ME

Winter Riddle

a haiku sequence

Things stick up through it.
Windshield wipers poke out and
Point up like antlers.

Thin orange stakes mark
The channel like buoys, a
Path for the oil guy.

Things stay above it.
Nuthatches hang upside-down
On the big white pine.

Blue Jays decorate
The bare branches of the old
Honeysuckle bush.

Things vanish in it.
Lawn chairs and garden sculptures,
Mourning Doves that land.

It muffles the stuff
You left outside into ghosts
Of what they were.

Things come after it.
Mais ou sont les neige d'antan?
All the poets ask.

When they have praised each
Present flake and are long gone,
New snow falls again.

Ashley Elizabeth Mitchell
Lincoln, ME

Tiger Lily

Blasts of fire
  Your orange overtakes
Bumblebees race to dig into your sweet nectar
    Carry more of your seeds to cover the lands
You bustle around
    Showing how tough you are
The long green stems put every flower to shame
    Magnificent piece of art
Your leaves dance in the wind
    The land is better than a ballroom floor
The Tiger Lily is more wild than free
    Tame is not in its nature
Tiger Lily needs no freedom
    It grows where it pleases
      You cannot stop it and you should not even try
        To try would give it freedom and take away
          the wild streak
Rebellious flower
    Vibrant important color
        Unappreciated colors and patterns
Land is here
    No restrictions
Blast of fire
    Pop up wherever necessary
You know where you belong
    And you are here to stay.

Robert B. Moreland
Pleasant Prairie, WI

Eastbound US-84

September afternoon, summer's last day,
drive the old Natchez-Vicksburg road, turn east
on Route eighty-four, memories flood back.
He's my hero; my uncle, Marine tough,
but even warriors get old. Honor learned
from Dad's best friend, both cut from the same cloth.
A Raider who at eighteen stood his ground;
Guam memories, shadowbox Silver Star
beneath Barbary pirates Corps saber.
Engineer, could have been a senator,
beloved patriarch; one weekend to spend.
Watched at the Audubon Café, as he
held court and walked back, looking like his dad.
My uncle for whom I am named grew weak
yet was embarrassed for me to see. So
I looked away or feigned distraction to
spare his dignity, his honor and pride.
Worked in his office for a bit, keen mind
teaching me engineering to do one
more job. Couldn't know if this was goodbye,
treasuring his "I love you" all the more.
Asphalt the color of corkboard stretches
westward, dissecting the towns of my youth.
We were immortal at sixteen, lost in
small town life, Dairy Queens and roller rinks.
Autumn dawns tomorrow, solstice of my
fifty-third year and as mortality
sneaks up, dappled sunshine filters in through
loblolly pines on red clay covered hills.
Silently, I thank God for this man, his
strong Irish Catholic wife; hope that my
life will make a difference, make them proud.

Cordula Mathias
Trevett, ME

Semper Fidelis

Your motto, not his.

You kept the faith.

In spite of all the lies,
You trusted him.

You brushed off
how many deceptions?

You made excuses
for his excuses.

You kept up
appearances.

You kept the kids and
kept the kids in the dark.

***

Sylvia Little-Sweat
Wingate, NC

Tulips

In Winter's late gray
Tulips lift their wine-glass stems
to toast new Spring green.

Elizabeth Lombardo
Walpole, ME

Out of Reach

I stare blankly in the dark. This is my first night alone in our new tent. The one that my sister and I were supposed to share. The night swims before my open eyes. I look hard, but everything is blackness. The campfire has been doused. The moon is absent. The night is still.

I turn my head to the left, sensing the emptiness next to me. My duffle bag is propped up against the far side of the tent, not at my feet where it would have been if my sister's air mattress was smushed up next to mine. I reach out my hand into the void, feeling the cold, empty space. My fingers close on nothingness. I can hear the shushing of the trees as the wind whispers past the full leaves of summer. It almost sounds like water rushing past, as though my tent is a rock in the middle of a river. Alone in our tent, I can't help but wonder: *Is this how it felt?*

***

It was the year that the snow didn't melt until May. We'd scheduled our kayaking trip for late June, but a few white patches still refused to surrender their places on the mountaintops, and the surrounding rivers were swollen with runoff. The rapids would be thrilling. Eyes bright with the anticipation of a thunderous ride, my sister and I loaded up the old tandem kayak and set out for the East Branch.

For a moment we were a part of the river, caught in the motion as it raced around rocks and made room for the unexpected turns. I caught my sister's smile as she turned her head back in my direction, proud to have joined in the rushing exodus towards the sea. The rock, unseen until we were already upon it, had not meant to stop us. It had always been there. But it was as if we'd stubbed a toe on an ancient

Elizabeth Lombardo
Walpole, ME

curb and bent over to nurse it amid a pressing crowd of people.

We flipped, enjambed suddenly between the rock and the drowned remains of a fallen tree, while the river kept on, unconcerned as it pushed its way past us.

Water frothed around us, lifting me out and pushing me down river, careless of the boulders it shoved me against, disregarding my sister as it trampled over her, not giving her room to breathe. I remember the angry rush against the current, the frantic scrambling up the piney shoreline, the impossibility of reaching her through the surge. The water held her under, until a careless spray dislodged the boat, the same way a foot aimlessly kicks a pebble free from a rut in the road. The chest compressions did nothing, her lungs already crushed by the weight of the watery masses.

***

My hand moves freely through the emptiness. At the end she must have been confused by the emptiness, too. Someone was supposed to be there for her, to grasp her outstretched hand. But I couldn't get to her. I lie in the darkness, feeling the weight of it crushing my arm, trying to pin me down. I breathe in and out, blindly watching my chest rise with the air that fills my lungs. *Was she aware of her breaths, as I am now? Did she watch her chest rise as she breathed in water, taking in death instead of life?* She was just beneath the surface. I'm sure she was watching, looking hard, with her fingers ready to grab hold. Like me. In the darkness, I look hard, wishing I could grab hold as I imagine my sister's shadowy presence slumbering peacefully beside me.

Peggy Trojan
Eau Claire, WI

Post Cards

Before cell phones,
travelers sent post cards.
My father always bought cards
on his business trips.
Mother found them in his suitcase
when he returned home.
She saved them in her scrapbook
with cards she got in the mail.
We have a pictorial record
of my father's trips.
We assumed he was having
a good time and wished
we were there.

***

The Swing

Pa made me a swing
from a wooden box.
Just big enough
for me and a doll or two.

If I stood and pumped,
I could swing for awhile.
Mostly, I was content
to sit suspended in shade
And my imagination.

Karen E. Wagner
Hudson, MA

The Thrill of It All

There's no comparison
to the thrill of my plunge
on the back of a Fleetwood Flyer
down car-lined, cobblestoned
Jillson Street. After the plows
made their first pass
when car tires just begin
to make hard-packed tracks,
out came the sleds.

I'd get off to a racer's start,
hit the ground with a clunk,
belly down, full layout
the length of my sled.
I perfected this approach,
(largely unchanged
through generations),
to eventually get the clunk
down to a soft whoosh.

It was easy to steer the sled.
Pull right on the crossbar
to go right, left to go left.
For the more experienced
there was also the use
of the toe on either boot
to act as a rudder.

Karen E. Wagner
Hudson, MA

Snow raced close
to my nose
as my chin rested
on the wooden slats.
Rutted ice crystals
and mini heaps
of clean snow
rushed before my eyes
that were open but blasted
by blown frigid flakes.
Blurred red eyes were
the hallmark
of a real sledder.

Is there room to let
the run play out before
it intersects
a busy boulevard
or should I head it up hill
and stop it short?
I can always drag the toes
of my boots to slow
the sled down too.
The best runs are
the fastest
and the longest
so I'm reluctant
to do anything to stop
the sled on purpose.

Karen E. Wagner
Hudson, MA

Days spent with my Fleetwood
Flyer were times
of unfettered joy
in an innocent young life
with no concept
of risk.

Oh for that feeling
of reckless abandon
it gave me.
Can I recapture it?
Or have age and sensibility
chased me completely
beyond reach of that thrill?

Whichever,
I have my memories
and can easily slink back
into them when I see
hills covered in fresh snow,
kids drag their coasters
uphill and hear that squeal
of rapture upon descent.
I'm pulled right back
to my City of Hills,
excitement ripples my spine
as I and my sled race
down cobblestones faster
than time speeds by.

Kristina Branch
Boothbay Harbor, ME

The Yellow Chairs

The first thing he noticed when he opened the door to the diner was that it was empty except for the woman behind the counter. Then he saw the chairs—all the same color—a deep rich yellow. It reminded him of the goldenrod behind the trailer where he used to live until the monstrous sheets of flame swept down the ridge and took everything he owned.

He didn't sit at any of the tables, but simply went up to the counter and ordered a cup of coffee. Standing there, he drank the coffee slowly, closing his eyes.

"That will be fifty cents," the woman said.

The man put down the cup. Digging into his shirt pocket, he found a few coins and slid them across the Formica. Two dimes, a quarter, two pennies.

"Close enough," the woman said, reaching out to scoop up the change. But then she tipped her head and scrutinized the man. Her hand drew back.

"You're my first customer today," she said. "The first one brings good luck." She pointed at the money. "No charge for the coffee."

One by one, the man picked up each coin, and as he did, he glanced around the diner. "If I may," he said in a careful voice, "The yellow...are you the one who chose it?"

"I certainly did," the woman replied tightly. "But it's worse for wear, I know." She sighed. "I can't do *everything* in this place."

The man walked over to a nearby table, studying the chairs. A few of them still looked fresh and glossy but others were scarred and scratched down to the wood.

"May I touch these up for you?" he asked. "I'm good at things like this."

The woman hesitated.

"No charge," the man said. "None at all."

Kristina Branch
Boothbay Harbor, ME

The woman drummed her fingers on the counter, and after a few long seconds she replied, “Wait here. I’ll get the paint. And then I’ll make you breakfast.”

As she turned away, the man sat down, removed his cap, and gently placed it on his knee.

Finally, he thought, *something in my life is going right.*

***

Gerald George
Belfast, ME

The Officer’s Revolver

Where were they going?
None of them knew, trudging over the road,
which maybe led to nowhere.
Asking the soldiers only got you
a rifle butt in the back,
and a curt remark.
Even the soldiers seem afraid,
as if they didn’t know either
whether a new labor camp lay at the road’s end
or a hidden ditch for killing.
However their officer knew.
You could tell by the way he kept his grim mouth shut,
motioning others out of the way when someone fell
so he could put a bullet in the prisoner’s skull.
He never holstered his revolver.
You had to keep your mind on something pleasant
if you could think at all,
or occupy your mind with an equation,
a conundrum, a poem.
Anything as long as it didn’t make you
stumble to the ground.

Ellen Taylor
Appleton, ME

Border Library

An invisible line separates Vermont and Quebec,
and here a library straddles the border.
Here, refugees sundered from family
by travel bans, reunite in this safe nest,
among cloth spines, Dewey Decimals and periodicals.
Two brothers separated by war, famine,
refugee camps: one wins a U. S. Visa lottery;
the other accepted only in Canada. An unlikely story,
but true. The faint flaking international boundary
line is painted in the hallway, between *Make Way*
for Ducklings, and *Good Night Moon*, where the brothers
and others, will reunite like pairs of birds,
share their stories of flight across the reading table,
their fledgling migration, a tale for our times.

***

Sarah Woolf-Wade
New Harbor, ME

From the Deep

Regrets are smooth round stones
tossed into a pond hidden in the darkened woods.
They sink in murky water to the bottom
forgotten for years in the mud
until, without warning, the water ripples,
the rocks transform to bubbles,
float through the moss to the surface,
burst unbidden
as unwanted dreams.

Susan Sklan
Cambridge, MA

The Other Side of Good-Bye

These nights I still sometimes find you.
You arrive through the doorway, your arms wide
open to me
and announce with a smile
that you have returned from your travels.
Are you Don Quixote after all?

I awake alone in the blue light
of early morning that wraps around me.
The silence is thrumming
and the hush of your absence is everywhere.

I tread the paths we took through woods,
over rocks that hug the sea.
Like the time we looked for Mars in the night sky.
Or when you showed me
a spiral of white stones laid out in a small field,
where you have to go backwards
in order to go forward.

***

My Son Returns to College After the Spring Break

The morning light is grey and soft
and through the window I can see the snow falling.
On the radio Diana Washington
sings "Trust in Me"
and the tulip leaves stand stiff
in the snow blanketing the garden.

Peter Daley
Belfast, ME

Ginny's Catch

Ginny was up early this cold January day. She and Jude were going ice fishing after breakfast. She hadn't spoken with him since Sunday but she was sure it was on. They had fished the pond together several times over the recent winters. She had watched his increasing enthusiasm for the sport. She loved the bracing cold, the flags set to stand alert by each carefully drilled hole, the desolate ice, and the remoteness of a Maine lake in winter when few people would be around to disturb the quiet.

Bristol Pond was not the largest body of water by far in Waldo County. It was ringed by mostly summer camps that were all vacant in the colder months. People from away with opulent homes in southern New England and even further afield opened their Maine vacation places in April and closed them back up in October. Pipes were drained and summer memories were packed away for winter dreams. Her father had one of the only year-round homes on the pond. He owned a local hardware store. No matter the time of year, people needed supplies. She had worked there since she was old enough to sort nuts and bolts. Ginny had no siblings. Her mother had left when Ginny was two. She had only a few, vague memories of the now distant woman. Daddy doted on his beloved Ginny. For her part, she was ready for a man of her own. Men were simple. She understood them. They usually did as she expected. Jude was simple that way and she especially enjoyed his company.

It would be their first time out on the ice this winter. December had been unusually warm and her work in the store had been busier than normal. The cold snap of the past two weeks had persisted with days below freezing and nights near zero. That, and a few good storms, established that winter had finally settled in. She had checked the ice on

Peter Daley
Belfast, ME

Saturday after work and Jude had agreed to come up this Tuesday to join her.

Ginny loved ice fishing. She was not a fan of the large groups that would spend weekends socializing and drinking, blaring loud music, or tearing about the pond on high powered sleds. She especially loved ice fishing with Jude. She liked being alone with him. He gratefully ate her lunches and praised her harmonica playing, never seeming to mind that she always caught the bigger fish. Even so, he was the storyteller of the couple. He probably told the best stories of anyone she knew. He made her chuckle without really seeming to try. It wasn't unusual for her to start laughing before he had gotten anyways near the funny part. She knew there would be a funny part—there always was with Jude. He had a nonchalant way of beginning: a strange thing had happened at work, or he'd had an interesting thought while he was waiting for his pants to dry at the laundromat. It always began with nothing much, but there was a certain way he spoke the words. He had a way of conveying merriment with his eyes. He never cracked a smile but the corners of his mouth might occasionally quiver as he contemplated the unfolding of the tale. She was his willing foil, listening intently, nodding and suppressing a giggle as he went on.

Ginny knew that Jude did not really share her passion for the ice. He was more of a city boy, but he kept her entertained and he brought her nice presents. He was the sort that women married. A junior accountant, he had grown up in Westbrook and had attended community college. After a short stint in the Navy, where he had learned about computer systems, he had settled into an ordinary enough life of sports fandom and collecting cars. His favorite was a yellow 1995 Corvette. She still had not driven that one.

She remembered earlier times together, too. There were the annual Christmas parties Dad's friend Steve held every year near Sebago. Jude was Steve's nephew and the only other ten year old in attendance that first year. They had

Peter Daley
Belfast, ME

been instant friends. Now, some fifteen years later, he had gotten a little drunk at the most recent party. He'd come on a little strong but, she had managed to deflect him all right. There would be plenty of time ahead for lovemaking. Men that mattered would wait patiently if you did just enough. She wanted Jude by her side. He was a good catch. He had a steady income and he gave her enough space. It was so great that he was making the two hour drive to join her today. She had stocked the ice shack with brandy and firewood, and prepared his favorite foods. She would reel him in slowly.

When he pulled into the dooryard around eight, it was in the turquoise blue CJ Jeep, the one that she had driven when they toured Baxter last summer. She recalled how they had been parked in a remote spot, looking across a grassy pond to where some moose had been feeding at the far edge. Without warning, a great blue heron had swooped down and perched just feet in front of the jeep. Jude had been so stunned he'd stopped his moose tale midway through the telling. They sat silently, afraid to spoil the moment. The heron had caught a medium-sized fish almost as soon as it settled its gangly legs. That was the day Ginny had begun to think of Jude as her own. He was a keeper. He would ask for her hand when the time was right. Of course, he would. The thought made her flush just a little as she sat relaxed with her second cup of Earl Gray.

Ginny was slow to notice that there were two people in the jeep. A young woman she did not recognize had just jumped out of the driver's side. They were already approaching the porch. Ginny opened the door wide to welcome them with the warmest smile she could muster. The whole day seemed to have changed in an instant. She was glad her father would not be around. He might be ashamed to think that his only daughter had to share the man she had chosen. Jude, after all, was a lucky little so and so. She had always kept a warm thought for him even while dating other boys.

Peter Daley
Belfast, ME

So what if a few had made it further upstream? It was Jude that she had decided on. She felt strangely now about this new disturbance in the calm waters of her being.

"Brooklyn" was bad news. It was her first time ice fishing. She had come along at Jude's invitation because she just *had* to see Bristol Pond for herself. Jude was winking as he had launched gamely into one of his silly stories about—what was it? Ginny was having difficulty concentrating. Brooklyn was chortling merrily about whatever the subject was. It was how they had met! Brook apparently worked at his gym. She certainly looked like the type. Her blond hair was tied in a tight little pony that waved behind her as she moved...She wore a little too much rouge over her already high cheeks. She had bony, hollow temples. Her lips were pouty. Her figure was less rounded than Ginny's but with a firmness of muscle that Ginny couldn't help but admire. She was impossibly petite and perky. She walked with a little swish of her hips. Jude was obviously interested. Ginny forced herself back to his story.

"...and Brooklyn just understood my fitness goals without my having to explain why I was focusing on my legs."

This was turning into an awful day. Was this Brooklyn into Jude? Why was she here? Which one of them thought this was a good idea? Brooklyn let out a short, bubbly burst of laughter, easily sliding an arm around Jude. His hand covered hers as naturally as a crow lands on a fish head tossed across the ice. Ginny wasn't feeling like herself. She smiled outwardly and brought the conversation around to the day's plan. There was fishing to be done, food and drink enough for three, and the Northern Pike would be biting. Did they have enough layers on? Ginny wondered if Jude could sense her disappointment. Bringing Brookie sweetie was a mistake. She would show him that. Ice fishing on Bristol Pond was *their* thing. Jude's and Ginny's. Brook trout did not belong. She'd probably wimp out by lunchtime.

"If you get cold, you can always come back to the house

to warm up," she said with diffidence.

"Oh, I love the cold! Jude and I have been snow shoeing together a few times since the last big storm. He usually tires before I do." Brooklyn poked Jude's side and he put on a grimace of pain.

"Ooof! She's kind of rough!" He faked a ridiculous expression while Brookie doll gritted her teeth, obviously enjoying the accusation.

"We'd better get moving. The fish won't wait." Ginny would not watch any more of this. Jude seemed different. She had resisted his more amorous advances. She could see now that she had miscalculated. There was still time to fix it.

"Arghh!" Brooklyn shrieked in real pain. They were all seated in the hut with the hole between them. A pesky fish hook had snagged her leg just above the ankle. Ginny scornfully wondered how this fitness witch had never learned to fish. Brook's pant leg had ridden up just enough for the hook to pass underneath, easily piercing her sock. A slight tug from Ginny had done the rest. Jude was all business now with the pliers. Brooklyn quickly recovered her composure and was sitting tensely still as Jude worked on the hook to free the barb from her skin. She winced as he backed it out, ripping a tiny chunk of tissue with it.

"I'm afraid that was my fault," Ginny ad libbed. "I pulled my tackle out from under your seat without much thought. I guess it caught on yours." Inwardly she was amused. Jude was no doubt sizing up the situation. On the one hand, there was Ginny with whom he had fished often and without incident. They knew each other's ways and the shack was perfect for the two of them. On the other hand, little Brookie was clumsy here, out of her element. She did not belong at Bristol Pond. He had to see that. "There it is." He held the hook up briefly and then set it to the side. "I'll head up to the house and grab the first aid kit out of the jeep." He sounded matter of fact but he flashed Ginny a look that she received with shock. It was angry reproach. Had he deduced that she had

Peter Daley
Belfast, ME

done this on purpose? She needed to refocus him. Ginny was the girl that drove his cars, that listened to his stories and that had poured attention on him at all of the right times. She had more than a keen interest in Jude. She had been actively leading him toward the ice these half dozen years. She knew he found her attractive. He could eventually have her. She had it all figured. She could have any local boy she wanted. She had proven that to herself already. She wanted Jude. She needed him to want her now. Today. She felt alarm taking hold. She reached for his arm.

"Be back in a flash." He hurried out of the shack.

The walk to the jeep and back would take him about ten minutes. He'd probably be running as much as he could over the slippery surface. Ginny turned back to Brooklyn who was looking down at her leg. It was only a slight wound and she was pressing her sock against it with her open palm. Brook didn't see the fillet knife before it crossed her throat, slicing deeply. She flopped helplessly onto the ice, gasping through the blood and writhing in agony, eyes wide with panic.

Ginny knew her way around a good fish.

Thomas Peter Bennett
Silver Spring, MD

Black Cherry in Spring

White petals falling
like snowflakes that drifted
from bare branches a month ago.

Olive-green leaves revealed
on branches that yesterday
were covered with white bouquets.

Dead branches
once camouflaged by
ivory floral clusters
exposed, revealing
a carefully attended squirrel's nest.

After winter winds and snow,
followed by cascades of
early spring rains,
a nest with carefully crafted
twig-and-leaf-thatched roof—
a beacon in the azure sky,
gleaming through an arch
between the two highest branches
of the black cherry tree.

From here, vigilant squirrels have
an aerial view
of the limbs above, below,
and in surrounding trees.

Cordula Mathias
Trevett, ME

Mother's Day

she wanted different things
and settled for less

less than she deserved.

it can't have been
easy for her:
        so much loss

her beloved brothers
both dead within two days
buried without a grave
in foreign soil

her father retreating
into his grief
his strength eaten away
by cancer

her mostly absentee
husband causing
discord
and disruption

in a life that
could have been
dignified
and serene

Cordula Mathias
Trevett, ME

her own mother
in constant pain
from arthritis, shingles, osteoporosis
and sorrow

her children
me included
selfishly
uncomprehending

***

P. C. Moorehead
North Lake, WI

Illumination

Like a meteor,
streaking across the sky,
love bursts in me
and casts an incandescent dust
into the depths of myself.

From that ground, the words come,
piercing, illuminating:
"Ah yes, I am Life.
Here, I am Life.
Do you hear?"

Steve Troyanovich
Florence, NJ

...in tattered twilight

for Amjad Nasser

the stranger has arrived
who has no yesterday or tomorrow
—Amjad Nasser

a dream
begins to cover
the shepherd's loneliness...
the star of the magi
neither warms the night
nor shelters against
tomorrow's despair

clutching the wind
childhood memories
slope towards emptiness...

at the edge of your shadow
the earth bleats

***

Sally Belenardo
Branford, CT

Haiku Q and A

What's the name of the
heron that's often put on
salad? Vin-egret.

Diana Coleman
Rockland, ME

A Memorable Encounter

We were Amtrak's "long haulers," cruising along in January from the West Coast headed east. Sitting in our seats, gazing out the windows at the passing snowy landscape, heads bowed over reading, or nodding off against the windows lulled to sleep by the clickety-clack of the steel wheels speeding along miles of tracks, we shuffled to the bathroom and dining car, and occasionally talked to our car mates. En route from Berkeley, California, I was headed to Washington, DC, for President Clinton's first inauguration in 1993. Wearing grey sweatpants, a turtleneck, wool sweater, and jeans, I sat with my winter parka draped over my lap, my backpack at my feet holding snacks in baggies—carrots, celery, and energy bars.

Slowly I woke up in my seat and moved my head around to relieve a stiff neck. Up at six one morning, I walked to the café with its expansive, pop-out, floor-to-ceiling windows to buy black coffee. I nodded to a thin, olive-skinned, brown-eyed man with wispy hair. He looked about seventy, and wore black pants and a white pressed shirt. Softly, he said, "Good Morning" as we waited for our coffees. As the train rocked back and forth, I carefully gripped my filled paper cup (which I'd save for washing my hair later in the railroad car's tiny metallic bathroom sink) and sat by a window in the café car. He took a seat across from me and smiled. We passed through California's Sierra Mountains, pine tree branches drooping with snow sparkling in the dawn's light. He was a violin-maker, originally from the Philippines, and lived in Los Angeles. He was going to deliver a newly crafted violin to a client in Chicago. In a whispery voice annunciating each word slowly, he said he loved his work, and came from generations of instrument makers. He enjoyed train travel to bring his violins to their destined musicians. He valued every

Diana Coleman
Rockland, ME

day he said. Grasping his cup with long, slender fingers, he looked at me with soulful eyes, shook his head, and said, "I don't understand how people can say they're *killing time*. Time is precious and should be treasured."

Whenever I hear others say they're *killing time,* I think of this gentle, talented, sweet man who created instruments to make beautiful music by violinists far and wide, and who would never utter those words.

***

Sylvia Little-Sweat
Wingate, NC

Water Music

Northward flows the Nile to the Mediterranean—
Iconic among rivers of the Globe, equally so,
Labyrinthine as the Ganges, Yangtze, Congo,
Euphrates, Amazon, Mississippi, or Rio Grande.

Rivers carve canyons, forge disparate cultures:
Irrevocable forces rushing headlong to the seas,
Vying landscapes for space, vitiating treaties.
Earth-and-all-Creation's penultimate reprieve, a
River's reprise through Pyramid Time to Infinity.

Patrick T. Randolph
Lincoln, NE

Winter Patterns

On your late evening windowpane,
Frost appears—you call it *Winter Patterns*—

Small frozen droplets reflecting Winter's emotions:
Excited loneliness, joyful sadness,
Blissful thoughts under a shade-tree,
A breeze-kissed summer afternoon—
Blue sky traveling into the endless night.

Staring into these *Winter Patterns,*
You gaze into the past and then walk hand in hand
Into the moment's now—

Tea kettle on the stove starts to boil.

***

Saturday Night Laundromat—1976

Old bachelor folds clothes—
A date with the midnight hour.
He stops, unfolds time;

Her hand, his cheek—that moment
At her sister's funeral.

Darrell McBreairty
Allagash, ME

Grande Armée

Word came today
that he had died
on that island
so far from France
and I could hear the sound
of marching boots
as we moved across the continent
with the wind at our backs
and the sun in our faces
and the sound of drums and the fife
leading us on into the evening.

There were so many tomorrows
as we buried our yesterdays
and clambered over hillocks
to the next victory
and the cheering of crowds
as we drank toasts
to our gallantry and youth.

With Moscow behind us
and the dust of Waterloo
a mere memory
we whisper in the shadow
of a time now lost
    and nearly forgotten
as someone plays a funeral dirge
on a broken pipe
retrieved from Borodino.

Helen Ackermann
Rothschild, WI

New Growth

We have a plant known as a dragon plant or more formally called Dracaena Margenata. We are attached to our plants but in many cases are not good at pruning them. In this case, the plant simply kept growing and soon was almost to the ceiling. We thought about parting ways but could not bring ourselves to let it die. Instead we did a sort of pruning. We cut the plant in half, putting the top half of it back into the soil and letting the other part simply stay rooted. I thought it looked forlorn. It seems the part put back in the soil formed new roots as it did not die but stayed green. The other part simply looked like a stick in the ground without any growth. One day, however, I noticed a great sprout coming out of the "stick." New life, new growth emerged.

This new growth gave me a sense of hope. During this pandemic time, I spent time struggling with anxiety and a loss of hope. I was not always positive. I missed so many things that gave meaning to my life; attendance in person at church, going to the Y, lunch with friends and hugging my grandchildren. New growth springing out of what seemed dead gave me a sense that perhaps I could sprout out in new growth. What was held deep inside my soul began to emerge and slowly I began to believe that I would experience new growth as well. Vaccinations emerged, the cases of Covid began to decrease and it seemed there was a light at the end of the tunnel. As many others, I evaluated what was truly important in my life and began to live in a different way. I concentrated on slowing down, living more in the present moment and enjoying nature by way of daily walks. I found myself being more attentive to the needs of others instead of focusing only on my own needs. I was sprouting new growth and with it a sense of gratitude for my many blessings.

Mary Jane Mason
Larchmont, NY

Flight

He stomped in the door, tracking mud, and sprawled in the rocker near the hearth.
She grabbed up her child from the floor, snatched her bag from the peg on the wall, and fled.
She ran until she thought she could run no more.
And still she ran. The sun set, her child shivered and cried and she ran.
In the moonlight, sheltered in a spruce grove, she peeled up moss and wiped the soiled child.
Ripping the hem from her long skirt she bound her bleeding feet.
The child nursed and they slept.
An owl's hoot woke her and she ran, stopping only to drink from a brook.
The high, hot sun shown down on the valley below.
She hid among rocks and watched.
The cabin looked peaceful.
He had not followed.
At dusk she stole silently to the back door and rapped softly.
The old woman's comforting embrace warmed her and the child.
She was home.

Matt Bernier
Pittsfield, ME

Fade Out

The last time I spoke to my aunt in Florida
she'd just come out of the intensive care unit
with a noise as if some assembly is required,
and I'm trying to learn why she's being moved

to another hospital, her breath heavy and rushed
as if she's on a curb waiting for a getaway car;
"Hospice, not hospital," she corrects me, adding
"Listen, I want my ashes spread on the lake,"

and there's a sound like wind through the pines
in front of her summer home, seconds hushed
like waves hitting a mossy boulder on shore,
and I promise, and tell her the family loves her,

and later that night I escape the din of a ticking
kitchen clock and stride out into the field,
where snow clouds gather, leaving a starry
hole in the sky where a meteorite briefly shoots,

and the next morning I'm not surprised by the call,
having known, after all, exactly when she passed,
startled by how quietly my mother's younger sister,
she of the folk generation, strummed the last chord.

Sylvia Little-Sweat
Wingate, NC

Italy

Eternal city—
Rome wears her antiquity
like a dusty cape.

The Coliseum—
ghosts of Gladiators whirl
to ghastly cries for blood.

Michelangelo
painting the Sistine frescos—
fame beyond his reach.

At the Spanish Steps—
nearby, the splashing fountain—
bier for poet Keats.

The cathedral tomb—
St. Francis of Assisi—
final dust at rest.

Tuscan sunflowers
turn yellow faces at dawn
to follow the sun.

Judith L. Braun
Alfred, ME

Christmas River of Memories

Every year a little after Thanksgiving, at the coming of the season of Advent, I approach the source of a river: "Christmas Memory Falls."

I anticipate with great excitement, as the first memory, is always the presentation of the Nativity Sets. The one from childhood with the plastic dime store characters, Jesus given at a church event, and a lamb that says Sunday School 1949 on the bottom! Somewhere, there is a picture of my sister and me kneeling in front of this scene, placed on the desk in the basement where we lived. I dreamed of creating a white mother of pearl ceramic Nativity. I did just that, at the Army craft shop on base in Germany where we lived at the time.

In case you are curious about the basement where we lived, I can attest it is true. Post WWII, when houses were being built, our family home was built on about two acres of land. The house was made of cement block basement walls. The upstairs was cement block surrounded by brick for the outer walls. The second floor was framed with rough (fuzzy) oak studs. I do not know the actual reason for not finishing. I make the assumption that there was not enough money, so we lived in the basement. One large room with a fireplace, served as bedroom at one end and "living room" at the other end where Christmas trees were placed. The other large room served as dining room and kitchen. The remaining room served as furnace, clothes storage and potty chair bathroom for my sister and me. My parents used a bucket. The contents were then dumped and buried in the back field.

Finally, I reach the river of free-flowing memories. Childhood pleasant memories of the neighbor's silver tin tree that rotated on a pedestal in their front window every year with pink and turquoise lights illuminating a mesmerizing sparkle. Our own LIVE tree growing out of a clump of dirt

Judith L. Braun
Alfred, ME

was set in the corner of the basement. No window there for others to see our tinsel glowing amidst the colored lights. Cousins tell me they remember the year my mother was obsessed with pink and turquoise plastic snowflakes hung from the ceiling joist in the basement as well as pink and turquoise lights on the tree! There was the year my sister and I received doll houses, metal, of course! We played "house" continually arranging and rearranging furniture. One year we kept the tree up until my birthday in February for our own private enjoyment! Each year, when we finally undecorated, it was moved to a permanent growing place in the backyard. Returning to the house many years later, we found those trees were about 30 feet high.

During the Christmas season aunts and uncles came to visit. My sister and I piled our gifts in separate places under the tree. There would be "show and tell" to the relatives. Seems we always had plenty of gifts. I remember my mother insisted that we open a Christmas Club account at the bank. I was given a card board holder with slots for quarters. This money, all $10.00, was spent on my family at the end of the year. In the 1950's ten dollars covered the family gifts. The ritual of saving for Christmas continues in my budget to this day.

Memories of the Christmases spent in Germany while my husband was stationed with the Army in Wiesbaden were full of new experiences. I loved the outdoor markets with delicious food, and learning about glühwein—a warm wintery holiday drink. It was in the markets that I developed a love of wooden trains. I started a collection with a very tiny one. It is about ½" high x 3" long. Over the years I have collected in excess of 30 wooden trains of varying sizes. Since returning to the States, I have included a tractor, a fire engine and other various items, all wooden. Military families are great at creating a "family" while overseas and I don't remember being lonely. We had plenty of parties to attend. I will always remember one particular Christmas tree as we thumb

Judith L. Braun
Alfred, ME

tacked a branch to fill out a bare spot. I believe this was the same tree when thrown over the third-story balcony, at the end of the season, landed with nary a needle left on it!

Returning to the States continues the flow of memories as we entered the stage of life with our own children. Shopping for gifts for them, baking cookies, decorating the house, inviting friends for parties, writing and sending a list of Christmas cards to friends, mailing packages to family. Our parents all lived in Ohio and I remember only one Christmas when my parents came before they passed and only one Christmas with my father-in-law visiting. There was so little in-person grandparent participation as my children grew up. To this day, this influences my adamant desire to be present for my children's children.

Now in my seasoned years with a bird's eye view of life, Christmas joy and "blue Christmas" are intertwined. My heart goes over the falls crashing against some rock as I remember the boyfriend relationship break up. This was the year my parents were hopeful that our engagement was a sure thing. They bought me a hope chest! The hope in that chest turned instead to tears. Smooth falling as I remember a few years later when we finally became engaged! My heart hit many rocks in the twenty-five years we were married. I crashed on the final one as we were divorcing during the holiday season. Like navigating around rocks in a river, my heart found the joy of smooth water, as I met a new guy. I traveled to Vermont at Christmas to meet his family. The next 15 years saw pleasant "blended family" memories as I balanced my own family and his for memorable gatherings. Alas, my heart hit another rock in the river, as we also were in the transition of divorce over the holiday season. At times, these anathemas have left me feeling excommunicated from love and life. I have learned they are just part of the flow of my river of life.

My current single life finds me using fewer and fewer of the decorations stored in boxes. I still bake or cook food for

Judith L. Braun
Alfred, ME

neighbors and send a few cards. Cards can now be sent in email, phone messenger, and online cards. My favorite is my own water color painting cards to send!

This Pandemic year I forged ahead in unpacking ALL the decorations, ALL the wooden trains, and ALL the wall hangings. I put up a small tree inside and decorated outside with hundreds of lights! Unwrapping all these memories just seemed to lighten the mood of this particular season.

This brings me further down the river, cruising along with the many memories of contributing to my grandchildren's Christmases. Their delight at all the gifts under the tree will remain long into the future.

It is JOY to my heart to witness my daughter and son continue some of the same traditions they grew up enjoying. My daughter prepares Christmas bread using the recipe that I used for Easter bread. Traditions now include what their spouses bring to the season.

As I float down this section of the Christmas river, the flow is slow as I pause to just "BE" in the midst of the joy and love of close family. I am looking ahead to the ways these grandchildren will celebrate in the years to come.

A journey over Christmas Memory Falls and down the river has taught me that where pools flow, curl back and dally are the most interesting, and the hardest to navigate. Hope, peace, joy and love are always present. Sometimes you just have to look for the one on the surface of the flowing current.

Jim Mello
Bucksport, ME

Wooden Shoes

So, we went back to the shell of a summer house
that bordered the pond
where we saw the mergansers and buffleheads
glide across the newly liberated waters.
To see the abandoned wooden shoes again,
that you love and would nurture.

You want them, fondle them, wrestle with the angel that
says—
"Take them home, they are slowly dying here."
On the second floor, near the old upright piano,
keys covered by shredding tar paper,
and that glass faced cabinet that you have already restored
in your ever firing imagination.

These shoes, which trigger iconic Holland, belong to you, I
believe,
rather than being left here to die of neglect,

like children in opiate addled homes,
like the marker stones in your secret cemeteries,
like the newly blossoming tree buds along the interstate
ignored by children passing by glazed by
the ubiquitous screens of electronica.

Jean Biegun
Davis, CA

Make a Joyful Noise

Make a joyful noise unto the Lord,
all ye lands.

—Psalm 100

My heart O God
You are Krazee Glued to.
Your carbon, your water, your

Electromagnetic beat charging
My little cells—
Nothing of me is apart from you.

Please help me make the kind decisions
To hate less,
To not be so lazy but bend to pick up

The plastic bottles at the beach,
And (better I know) not buy them at all.
Through small glimpses of you

May I piece together more of your
Cosmic sensibility. Help me climb
The tallest ridge to touch the hem of your

Starry robe. Unclog my ears so I
Understand the sermons of the microbial
Diatoms testifying in my patchy backyard

As to your complexity. That family
At the edge of the water, a son and daughter
Posing for photos as I watch from my car

Jean Biegun
Davis, CA

In the lot—you are in their chemical
Bonding and likewise within those waves
Beyond them hailing:

We have rolled all this way on the breast
Of the Lord, so sing to us now loud
Anthems of joy as we high-five you!

***

Julie Babb
Damariscotta, ME

The Monarch

Does the Monarch know
As he flashes his orange exuberance
From one frenzied beach rose to the other,
How far he will have to fly
To stretch, hourly draining strength
From his failing wings.
Only to reach a dry and ocean-less land
Which will cost him his life.
Does he know why he makes his sacrifice?
Does he know God?

Sally Belenardo
Branford, CT

The Ants' Reward

Shears in hand, she walks slowly between rows
of the peony bed, choosing a few
of each variety. Here are cream ones, edged
with softest pink, their heady fragrance
inhaled as a memory evermore;

here are spheres of deep rose, and snowy white ones
with traces of crimson in the center. There,
dark burgundy ones, petals burnished by sun.
Seemingly made of ruffled feathers,
nevertheless they weight the stems.

Quickly she takes them to the house,
lays them on the kitchen counter. To prolong
the life of the bouquet, she removes any leaves
that would decay under water in the vase.
But now, to her dismay, some ants

she displaced from the garden seek
shelter in the unnatural surroundings,
the ants that ate away the waxy covering
that seals peony buds shut. Without them
the flowers would've failed to open.

The ants, captured in the bristles of a scrub brush,
are swept into the slippery sink, try to climb
the sides to no avail, mortally wounded
and those surviving still, forced down
the drain in scalding torrent.

Jane Ross Potter
Bar Harbor, ME

A Year of Moments

An unexamined life is not worth living.

—Socrates

Jennifer's version of examining her own life consisted of keeping and re-reading a series of journals. She'd maintained this practice for decades, and was now at that age, not a specific age but a subjective age, a time when one looks both ahead and back. Ahead to wondering what will become of one's possessions upon death, and back, wondering what someone else reading the journals would think of her. It was one thing to examine her own life, but having it examined by others was a different matter.

Now, personal journals and journal-editing paraphernalia were arrayed on Jennifer's worktable. Evidence of a life well-lived (she hoped), the journals were all hand-written. Colorful ribbons, tag strings, and other non-paper ephemera extended beyond the pages; the overall effect might be untidy to critical eyes, but made it easy for Jennifer to find a specific memory.

In various sizes, widths, and designs, the journals stood in chronological order between two bookends. On the right side of the table, editing tools were arrayed like surgical instruments: containers of white-out to conceal secrets; scissors large and small to excise moments best forgotten; tape to heal between the excisions; and sticky notes on which to write instructions for future action, for post-surgical care. Journal-editing had become a regular feature of Jennifer's life, once she overcame her reluctance to, in effect, rewrite her own history.

Some entries she'd prefer not to read again: upon examination, certain events were best left in the past where they belonged. On a recent editing spree, she'd distilled one year into two typed pages (films seen, trips taken), then promptly

Jane Ross Potter
Bar Harbor, ME

shredded the original pages that were covered with her handwriting of three decades ago. The shredder teeth, with their high-pitched grinding, reduced all evidence of... well, it's confetti now, so why mention it again.

Over time, she developed a clearer idea of what to keep and what to cut out, tear out, or white-out, depending on how much she'd written at the time. Some journals only needed a light touch: plastic surgery, a nip and cut here and there, nothing major. A few entries were incomplete, with phrases like, "had dinner at [blank] with three people from work..." or "saw concert with really good English conductor [blank]." Obviously, she'd meant to go back and add the missing information, but days, weeks, months went by, and now she was left scrolling through emails to see if there was a record of making the dinner plans.

She did eventually track down the missing conductor's name, by checking his schedule online. Whether that added to the journal's value was questionable, but the blank spaces would bug her future self, so this was gift to that person. The missing pieces had become a bit of an obsession, and she vowed going forward not to leave blanks that could be more efficiently completed at the time of writing.

The journals up through the end of 2019 were so full of ephemera that life itself seemed to burst from its paper confines: concert tickets, photographs, small pictures clipped from programs, train tickets, and found objects placed in small clear adhesive envelopes. The ribbons were loosely interleafed and marked receipt of a gift, or from a favorite bakery, even from a box of chocolates. One envelope preserved and protected a tiny Origami paper crane, a gift from a performer after a memorable Japanese drum performance, a complete memory enfolded in a tiny scrap of paper.

Jennifer sat at the table and paged through the recent journals to make sure there were no more missing words, placenames, photographs, or other issues that would prevent the journal from being declared "complete" and placed back

Jane Ross Potter
Bar Harbor, ME

on the shelf. That done, she took a deep breath and picked up the next journal, the one for the year 2020. She could hardly bear to open it, so she put it down again while she made a cup of tea. Then, sighing deeply, she got back to work.

Reliving 2016–2019 had taken her on a whirlwind of travel stretching from Paris to Venice to Tuscany, then up and down the British Isles, a quick trip to Holland for the tulips, and at least twelve U.S. states plus Canada. But when she stepped into her journal of 2020, a mental cloud descended and all motion seemed to grind to a halt. Reading the journal evoked the sense of confinement the year had imposed, both physically and mentally.

Partway into 2020, she had realized that the journal only contained her handwriting; missing were the French bakery box ribbons, the photos of interesting architecture, the smiling, mask-less friends leaning close so they could all get in the picture. 2020 so far had no found treasures in little clear pockets, no theater tickets, no film house stubs, no business cards of places to revisit, no exhibition pictures cut from museum pamphlets, no cute notes from friends. 2020 was becoming a thin journal, documenting a life lived at home, on screen.

Around March 2020, when she'd cancelled all her upcoming travel for the next several months, she knew it was time to get creative or her journal would turn into one long and difficult narrative. So, camera at the ready, she began documenting the strange and tragic year. A group video call for someone's birthday? Take a screenshot for posterity. A distant friend emailed a photo of her boyfriend's dog in its birthday hat? Print and add to the journal, never mind that she'd never met the boyfriend, let alone the dog.

She photographed the snow on the trees, she took pictures of herself outdoors in a variety of masks, she photographed handcrafts she made during lockdown. Days when she had physical therapy at the hospital for a broken

Jane Ross Potter
Bar Harbor, ME

arm were marked with little round smiley-face stickers showing Covid-19 screening: more tiny scraps of paper to mark an era. A box of Godiva chocolates supplied a single much-needed red ribbon. She inserted quotes from books she read.

By the end of 2020, her journal was outwardly much like the previous years...okay, it only had one piece of ribbon, but it was full of memories. The in-person visits might be missing, but the video calls made sure she was up to date with her close family and friends. And one advantage was that on screen you are mainly seen from the front, so she got away with her self-haircuts.

From the many Zoom courses she took (dutifully documented in the journal), she learned a lot about astronomy, mosaics, mystery writers, and various esoteric subjects she'd never thought much about. She reached December 31 without catching the virus, for which she was very relieved, and experienced the New Year's festivities on screen, just as she had lived most of the year.

The journal for 2021 begins on a positive note, with a masked, socially distanced walk with friends, and the entry for New Year's Day also contains the first find of the year, a lucky dime picked up during the walk, and now secured in a little clear envelope to punctuate the day. She has an overseas flight booked for later in 2021, and is looking forward to filling the journal once again with travel mementoes, photos of friends old and new, and tickets from live performances. Only time will tell.

Meanwhile, she can lighten the journal's mood with more signs of an era. The Lawyer who was not a Cat, marked in the journal with a couple of screenshots of the kitten-filtered lawyer on Zoom, the kitten looking more anxious by the moment. A cartoon from England providing some comic relief from the latest lockdown, in which a sign announces Tier 4 Restrictions: "Roast potatoes may be on the same plate as bread sauce, but they can't meet up with turkey. Sprouts must self-isolate."

Jane Ross Potter
Bar Harbor, ME

When she looks at her 2020 journal, with its lonely solitary ribbon, she has mixed feelings. It's a year she would like to strike off the calendar, reset the clock to December 31, 2019, and have a do-over. But there is also true gratitude that she lost no loved ones to the terrible pandemic: in this she knows she is very lucky. And although she could do without the year itself, she wouldn't exchange the precious moments of connection it contained, the memories of special events shared over video calls and across time zones. Regardless of how many times she examines 2020, this journal will never need white-out.

***

Mary Ann Bedwell
Grants, NM

Friends with Benefits

He crosses the room as I lay reading,
Softly as though not to wake.

Gently he lies down beside me,
His body conforming to mine.

As he stretches alongside,
I feel his warmth penetrating my body.

I pull his head to my chest,
Stroke his soft hair.

He nuzzles my neck as
I relax into his embrace.

My brother knew I needed a cat!

Grace B. Sheridan
Cutler, ME

Observing a Desk

On the fourteenth of November
the Christmas cactus from Jeannie
in the rose pot on the landing
arches forward.

Two pink blossoms like pastel birds
peer down at cousins on the desk:
a lady slipper in the wild
photographed by Dawn, a painting
"Tulips in Tinware" by Christine.

Near each five by seven card
a smaller pitcher—one creamy
with slanted sides, pixie-eared handle,
sleek curved spout as if custard sauce
is pouring over Mother's snow pudding;

The squat one, glossy pale green,
its full view hidden from this chair
by the antique teapot from Ireland
which Kelly, in her final days,
insisted must be mine. The crocheted mat
on which it sits, a ruffled frame.

Off and on the sunshine breaks through,
highlights the grain of the maple
or the original pulls on the drawers
stuffed with placemats and tablecloths
rarely used any more.

Grace B. Sheridan
Cutler, ME

The furniture buyer made an offer
but I'm not ready to sell. The blossoms
will enjoy observing the desk
for yet a few days longer.

***

Steve Troyanovich
Florence, NJ

the silent and the alone

for Anna Akhmatova

let the lost light not mock
the river that does not flow
cradled in the stillness
of another empty moon...

your lips spoke
like petals of death
perfumed wildflowers
now blooming beneath the dusk...

into an empty mirror
blazed the red eyes of summer
soon replaced
by autumn's rustling breath...

i wait for you...in that constellation
of darkness...no angel's choir
to sing...only the silent and the alone.

Bill Herring
Minnetonka, MN

Summer School

—for Sharon

She has the power to stop the world
on its axis for no other reason
than to have her gardeners stop
what they've been doing, look around
and admire the doing they've just done.

It's late May, and this patch of the planet
is shape-shifting into mystical June,
the month of the rose. Golden Celebration.
Breath of Life. Angel Eyes. New Dawn
and Night Owl, Starlight Symphony
and Twice in a Blue Moon.

This is a woman lost in a love affair
with nature and being outdoors
with her gardeners. College students
away from the dorm, the books, the campus
and into her classroom, where she teaches
the language of Chinese bellflowers,
the literature of cardinal red geraniums,
the poetry of deep purple salvia
and Endless Summer blue hydrangeas

***

September Canvas

Frogs bedded down now.
Sky's lettered with V's of geese.
Time to paint the trees

Amie McGraham
Scottsdale, AZ

Subdivided We Stand

Not long ago, I knocked at a house down the street. Next door, a dog with a neck the size of a tree trunk stood guard. He wouldn't let me near him and I didn't want to scare him off. But I had to wonder: *Is this his house?* and then: *Where are his people?*

"There's a giant yellow Lab standing in your neighbor's driveway," I said to the man who finally answered the door after five minutes of yapping Chihuahuas and multiple raps on the etched glass-and-mahogany door. I have the same front door, I noted, a nod to the late eighties when this subdivision was built. Half a dozen dead poinsettias, caked with the dust of another rainless year, stood beneath the empty spot where the doorbell was at my house.

"Do you know if he lives there?" I asked. "Ever seen him around the neighborhood?"

The man's features seemed blurred, somehow, as if he were being erased. Vacant eyes, gray and hollow, like my mother's these past few years. Behind him, a Christmas tree. *It's almost Valentine's Day,* I thought, *really?* A year into the pandemic and time's passage remained distorted, fluctuating between dog years and days lasting for months.

"Nope," he said, inching the door shut. An etagere with multiple shelves of glass figurines leaned precariously against the sliding china door. "Never seen a dog around here."

"He won't leave that driveway," I continued, like: I know, I just *know* the dog must have somehow escaped his yard or house and was now waiting patiently for his family to come home. "He must live nearby?"

The door slammed and I returned to the dog in the driveway. He was still wary of me, standing well beyond the six feet of obligatory social space we've all been forced into this

Amie McGraham
Scottsdale, AZ

past year. I spent a few minutes reassuring him that he was, indeed, a good boy, but he was skeptical and retreated closer to the house.

Next door, the door opened again and out came a couple: the blurry guy and a frumpy woman.

"Is it..." the blurry guy began.

"Yup! It's Cashew!" A dishwater blonde, white T-shirt gone gray, pink flip flops.

The Lab—Cashew—perked up when he saw her. "Where's Eric?" she asked the dog. "Where's your papa?"

I asked her if she had Eric's number, because what if he's gone all weekend? Did the dog usually wear a collar? Did he often get loose? Did she know Eric's last name?

"You know how it is," she sighed. "I know Eric, but I don't know Eric. I mean, yeah, he's my neighbor, but...."

I knew exactly what she meant. Subdivisions are nothing like where I grew up, on a small Maine island three thousand miles away. On the island, we all knew each other, we'd all lived in our centuries-old houses for generation upon generation and even if there were five acres between us, we knew: who you were; if you lobstered or waitressed; if you ran the bakery or drove the snowplow; if you preferred black raspberry ice cream to maple walnut; the last four digits of your landline.

"Yeah," I said, "I don't know my neighbor's last name either, and I've lived here twenty years." I didn't mention the neighbors on the other side of the cinderblock wall, who moved in a few years ago. We've exchanged occasional waves—he, usually sporting plaid sweatpants, she in hijab—but I don't even know their first names.

"That's gotta change," she said. "Especially these days." She gestured toward the sky, as if the heavens held our future. "I'm Joyce, by the way." She smiled and patted the dog. "I'll see if I can at least get him into our backyard. Eric's is padlocked."

I walked down the street toward my house. Cashew

Amie McGraham
Scottsdale, AZ

retreated to his front stoop.

I've been a dog lover ever since my family adopted the black fringy mutt named Jack who became the four-legged sibling to my only-child self. Many more dogs, pet-sitting clients and animal shelter volunteer hours followed, so naturally I was concerned and returned that evening to check on Cashew. Had Joyce been able to corral him? Was his family back yet? Was he still protecting his fortress? The twin lanterns flanking Eric's garage shone brightly; I took this as a hopeful sign. I rang the doorbell, and from the other side of the etched glass-and-mahogany door, a dog barked.

The door opened and Cashew bounded out, sashaying between my legs as if he'd known me for years. The dog treats I'd brought over earlier remained untouched, three steps down. The air was heavy with the aroma of burgers from a nearby barbeque.

"Hi...Eric? I live up the street," I began. "Just checking to make sure Cashew's okay." The dog nuzzled my hand. "Sorry to bother you—"

"No bother at all," Eric said, adjusting his Diamondbacks ball cap. "I appreciate the follow-up." He looked like one of my Maine neighbors: flannel shirt over a gray thermal, thick beard, work boots. "We can't figure out how he got out. Our gate was locked, the garage was closed, the front door was locked...."

It occurred to me then that, in our subdivisioned parcels, we're all a bit like Cashew: guardians of our own galaxies, afraid of opening the gates of our castles to allow anyone in. And in this strange pandemic space we've collectively orbited for well over a year now, fear of the invisible enemy who shares its name with a brand of beer has caused even more isolation. Masked and distant, we tiptoe around human contact, instead choosing self-checkouts or grocery delivery or curbside takeout, yet all the while desperately craving interaction. Pandemic or no pandemic, we remain sequestered within the walled safety of our subdivisions, separated from our cities and communities, detached from our own selves.

And I am here, finally settled in the same city, the same house, with the same partner for two decades, a monumental milestone representing the longest I have ever remained in one spot. I have finally conquered the alcoholic wanderlust that led me from one coast to another, to foreign countries, through multiple jobs and shattered relationships.

Yet I do not know my neighbors.

Last summer after a three-month lockdown, I returned to the island of my childhood. To escape the pandemic and Phoenix with its bland similitude, the days as monochromatic as the stuccoed subdivisions in this crispy, sepia-toned desert. To escape the cloaked anonymity of the nation's fifth largest city that had suddenly become the global hotspot for COVID deaths. To visit my mother at her memory care home, where I learned to embrace her dementia, even if we had to be ten feet from each other, outdoors and masked. To celebrate my father's 88th birthday, foregoing FaceTime for lobster rolls and homemade blueberry gingerbread, still warm from the ancient Hotpoint oven in the tiny kitchen where my mother created culinary masterpieces so long ago. Together, on the back porch overlooking the sea.

I returned to the island and was pleasantly surprised to find the sense of community I had known so well largely unchanged by the pandemic. The island, with its six hundred souls and one case of COVID. The island, with its three-room schoolhouse I attended for eight grades. The island, where even fifty years later, nothing much had changed. On the island, I didn't dream of a return to normalcy, because normal had never left.

I came back to the desert last fall, to the unforgiving glare of rock lawns, the sharp-edged thud of sunset, the cloying chalky smell of hot concrete. Re-entry was difficult: angry people, angry elections, angry weather. People celebrated holidays in ridiculously large groups. The virus surged through Arizona, not just once but twice more. Vaccines

Amie McGraham
Scottsdale, AZ

have not yet replaced masks. Occasionally humankind is both again.

And still, I do not know my neighbors.

My mother passed away recently; my days waver between what was and what is. I have inherited our old island farmhouse and enough sorrow to fill the cove that surrounds it. I have inherited her passion for the simplicity of island life. It took death to bring her home, in a box of dust and bone. Her aura permeates every barnboard bookshelf and cedar clapboard of the house where she lived for fifty years. In this house, on this island with the islanders, is where I truly feel at peace.

But, still the desert: A husband, two dogs, a cat and another house.

Inhabiting two worlds is tricky. The longer I remain out west, the more vast the divide between us grows, and her image becomes the fading wisp of a falling star. Some days all I want to do is escape—the pandemic, the desert, life itself. And some days, I cling to the shimmery dream of the final move home.

***

Robert B. Moreland
Pleasant Prairie, WI

Tenacity

Large green apple leaf
moving steadily forward
powered by an ant.

Moreland, R.B. (2014) 2015 *Wisconsin Poet's Calendar*, page 52.

Genie Dailey
Jefferson, ME

Courage

Brave little soldiers
at attention in the snow—
silly daffodils!

***

Convicted

Crow triumvirate
judges my dereliction.
I fill the feeders.

***

Aromatic

Stop—smell the roses!
So goes the admonition.
But oh! Balsam fir!

Ilga Winicov Harrington
Falmouth, ME

Distracted in Cuba

Sally sat and stared at her boarding pass, oblivious to the clutter of the airport waiting room. Havana? What had she let Deena talk her into this time? Or was she running away?

Their group was busy sorting out various suitcases, personal and donated items, waiting to be checked in for their flight. Deena's friend David had organized the tour. They were traveling under the auspices of a "humanitarian mission," as travel to Cuba by Americans was technically forbidden under normal circumstances. The year was 2006 and there was a single American Airlines flight per week from Miami to Cuba, leaving on a Saturday morning with a return flight the following morning. The crew included a mechanic and spare parts, since the estrangement between US and Cuba precluded local airplane service.

Deena strode back from the ticket counter: "Did you check your big suitcase? We're allowed only one carry-on and a purse equivalent." She spoke in her courtroom lawyer voice, certain of all her facts.

Sally nodded and offered a vague smile, "Uhum...."

Deena frowned as she assessed Sally's uncertain countenance, "Are you still debating about that relationship and sifting the evidence? Get over it. This is supposed to be fun."

"I suppose it will be a distraction."

"No kidding! You should have heard David and Alvaro going toe-to-toe with security about all the luggage. Never mind that most of the suitcases are full of drugstore items for common ailments and even incontinence pads. Fortunately, David's wife used her diplomatic skills and we're set to go."

The flight landed at José Marti airport in Havana. The island had a new modern airport, but it was decreed unavailable to American planes. Mid-May was hot and steamy; they sat for hours waiting to be processed by security. Deena was

Ilga Winicov Harrington
Falmouth, ME

singled out, along with a couple of other lawyers in their group for special questioning. Apparently, anyone practicing law was not a welcome visitor, regardless of an association with a humanitarian cause.

A couple of surly officials examined their papers with a frown. When they spied a wheelchair among the luggage, David casually guided a teen daughter traveling with the group to sit in it.

The guide Alvaro explained with an ingratiating smile, "Señorita is most unfortunately weak and cannot walk on her own."

The clever girl did not miss a beat and collapsed in the chair, letting her head droop. Her mother patted her arm and took hold of the handles. Everyone was allowed to pass. When the bus departed for the Swedish built hotel, everyone breathed in relief.

The following week would bring contradictions at every turn; their hotel was modern and air-conditioned, but only for foreigners. The sparse traffic sported a mix of shiny chrome on cars shaped back in the 1950's, but most were likely held together with wire and home-made parts. There was incredible and joyful music everywhere, but the old elegant houses had become tenements. The threadbare neighborhood Cuban markets ran on allotted stamps, but others were overflowing with colorful produce which could be bought only with American dollars. The government openly supported the two-tiered economy, the stream of US dollars flowing from expatriates in Florida.

Their small group of fifteen, always accompanied by an official Cuban guide, spent days exploring Havana. They made two deliveries of their "humanitarian goods" to the Catholic Caritas and Jewish Charity Homes respectively. State support was minimal for these organizations and they were most grateful for such deliveries, the wheelchair being an unattainable luxury.

The group spent one delightful morning at the Lizt Alonso

"Dance Cuba" music school and watched a special dance performance that the school hoped to promote to US through an arts exchange program. Another day Sally and Deena went to visit the old Hemingway estate "Finca Vigia" that was under restoration. It was hot and dusty. The restoration had just started on the house, which was closed to visitors, so they wandered the gardens. The swimming pool where Ava Gardner and Hemingway entertained Hollywood friends was empty and full of palm fronds. His wooden 40 foot cruiser was still there, but the place was overrun with mangy dogs. It was depressing. Sally looked down as they departed, trying to avoid tripping on the debris-strewn walk.

Just like my life she thought. There is too much baggage for restoration. She had such young hopes: all things seemed possible when she and Sam had married. She was a small town girl just out of college, and Sam was already a man of the world with a good job in the banking industry. Early on, they had laughed and danced, enjoying their union, the ease of boundless horizons. Their son Robin was born before their one year anniversary. They should have settled in as a family, but Sam found domestic boundaries restricting. They had limped along for ten years. Sam came to drink more and more and then one day came the crash and he was dead.

They were not financially destitute, but her world had fallen apart. Like this place, her former sense of purpose was lost. Still, they had survived. She had gone back to school to become a physical therapist and now years later, Robin was in college. She was proud of the young man he had become, but with the exception of friends like Deena, her day-to-day routine had grown suffocating, until a couple of months ago.

Deena's arm folded around her, "I always thought he was too tough on women in his books. *Sic transit gloria!*" In a grand sweep she thrust her arm in the air around them.

"It is hard to imagine what this was like in his time," Sally slowly responded as she came out of her musings.

A short distance from the Hemmingway estate they found

Cojimar, the town where he wrote "The Old Man and the Sea." The story reminded them that the value of an encounter itself might be more important than the final outcome, and lunch at the seaside restaurant with flavorful seafood restored their spirits.

Private restaurants in Havana proper were another anomaly. Most restaurants were state owned, but paladares, small officially licensed restaurants, were independently owned. Most were found in private homes. One evening with no scheduled activities, a couple from the group asked Deena and Sally to join them in exploring the restaurant Las Garritas. The paladar was acclaimed not only for its décor and food, but also the movie "Strawberries and Chocolate" with Marilyn Monroe had been filmed there. A taxi took them down a narrow back street and stopped in front of a four story building. It required a climb to the 3rd floor, past balconies and stairways hung with drying laundry like ghosts of the past. The pervasive odor was mold.

After knocking they were welcomed to a most eclectic Victorian salon. Plush maroon velvet drapes shut out the world and crystal glistened on white tablecloths. A huge statue of a wounded and bleeding Jesus in the Spanish style overshadowed their table. On the other side of the smallish room was a grand bookcase displaying old photographs of Marylyn Monroe. They all took a deep breath and relaxed into a make-believe world with pricey savory food and patrons dressed with subtle elegance not seen on the streets.

This was quite in contrast to another dinner. Someone had suggested Don Lorenzo to Deena and Sally as an unusual place. They lacked a house number and could only provide a street name. Their taxi driver shook his head. This part of town was known for its warren of streets where names and numbers changed on a whim. When they finally arrived after navigating up and down several alleys; the driver got out, locked the car with Sally and Deena in it and went to check if they would be safe there. Returning, he pronounced it "small but good" and followed them in, probably to receive a tip from the owner for bringing American clientele. This dining area was on the rooftop on the third level, a ramshackle apartment building across the street. They were certainly out of the tourist area. The owner, in rudimentary English walked them through an extensive menu at their table overlooking the street.

When it started to rain, heavy raindrops lent a staccato rhythm to their meal beneath the corrugate metal sheets that constituted the roof. A leak appeared between the metal sheets and bare sagging wires strung with lights went out above them. A large waiter sauntered over and calmly reconnected them with his bare hands. Across the street another electrical box flared out from the deluge. It was just another night on an island seemingly held together with duck-tape. Despite the rain, Deena pronounced the daiquiris perfect. Fried banana and pungent meatball appetizers were followed with fish in almond sauce, some lamb and brown rice and salad. They received some strange looks from the other patrons, but the general atmosphere was happy as was the owner, since they were obliged to pay in American dollars. They left as they had arrived. The owner called a cab, making them wait upstairs until the cab pulled up to the door and then personally escorted them down to the taxi.

When they got back to their hotel room, both women flopped in their chairs laughing.

"Wasn't that an implausible dinner?"

"Indisputably!" Deena grinned and then casually added, "Don't you wish you could have shared this with Brian?"

Sally took a deep breath and pinched her lips. The topic of Brian had been off-limits since they arrived in Cuba and Sally was not ready to discuss it out loud. *Not only had she thought about him at dinner, but countless other times every day. Except that every time it happened a fog of fear enveloped her and internal cautioning from the past echoed in her mind.*

Ilga Winicov Harrington
Falmouth, ME

Deena had introduced Brian McKinney to her at a party several months ago and they had immediately developed a friendship that now had the potential of becoming a lot more. Brian was an architect, widower with a grown son, wished for a stable home life and had pursued that conversation with her last month. And Sally was afraid! She had become comfortable in the last ten years with her days of calm and predictable cadence with work and friends for company. But she was lonely, now that Robin was away. And Brian had certainly made her feel alive once again.

"I don't want to talk about it."

Deena was relentless, "You have to! This trip was supposed to give space and time to resolve your insecurities."

"I'm trying, but every time I start, there is that foggy wall before me and I can't seem to think."

"What's so hard? You certainly have feelings for him, he is a good looking mature man, quite responsible and willing to consider your needs. What is more, he asked you to marry him, which these days seems a novel approach," she said with a harsh laugh. Deena had her own decided opinions regarding men, construed from her past experiences.

"Deena, but that is what scares me. I didn't do so well considering such things the first time. People change. Can I trust him to remain warm and caring?"

And she remembered all Sam's unexpected outbursts and unexplained business absences. During those years she had become quite adept at rearranging last-minute social events and explaining to Robin once more that his father would not be able to attend his game.

Deena yawned broadly, "Well, maybe you just need to have an affair with him and leave it at that. I'm going to bed. Tomorrow is likely to be a long day."

"How can you be so crass and blunt about this? Were you never a romantic, or am I a relic of the past?"

"Probably! I gave that up years ago as delusional. Good night."

Ilga Winicov Harrington
Falmouth, ME

Sally turned in as well, but sleep eluded her for some time.

David, their tour organizer, was much interested in Art Deco architecture prevalent in Havana. After a lecture, the group set out to visit the "House of Friendship," a huge old Art Deco mansion, abandoned by the original owner and taken over by the government for a museum. The officially repudiated opulent lifestyle of its former wealthy owners, now likely living in Miami, was preserved incongruously.

Reconstruction of architectural gems seemingly limped along elsewhere in Cuba. A bus trip to Boyeros, in the outskirts of Havana, led them to a historic Art Deco movie theatre. It was built in collaboration with Paramount Studios in the early 1930's during the Machado era. The lobby, partially restored, featured a painting of wild-eyed Dali, as well as prominent displays of pop-art. The rest of the building was an unmitigated disaster.

"This is incredible," said Deena as they peered inside the dilapidated theatre.

Many of the seats were broken and long cobwebs swayed eerily from the partially open curtain on the stage.

"All this architectural sightseeing makes for a depressing distraction," Deena teased Sally.

"Yes and no," Sally shook her head. "It's not Brian's style."

"Oh! I think you are making progress! You are willing to talk about him in conversation," Deena chuckled as they left the theatre and stepped out in the bright afternoon sun.

The following morning, their group continued to play tourist. First came the state-owned Corona Cigar Factory, where everything, even the cigar boxes were hand crafted. They were proudly told that each employee was given several cigars a day, depending on quality of their work and position in the factory. Someone from their group speculated that the cigars were a backhanded form of extra pay.

Then through Miramar to Jaimanitas and the

studio/enclave of José Fuster, the famous tile artist. They gaped at the compound constructed entirely of hand-painted artistic tiles.

"It's as bad as Portugal!" exclaimed Deena.

"Bad? I thought you liked tiles?" In fact, Sally had seen some in Deena's kitchen.

"Yes. But not kitsch. Well, maybe it's not all..." Deena picked up and inspected a red tile and headed to a different room.

Left alone, Sally stood in front of a long table displaying tiles with various aquatic themes. *Her thoughts had drifted to Brian. He liked to fish and had even made a dinner for her once with some fish he had caught. It had been such a warm and homey evening. Without thinking,* she reached for a set of six small tiles arranged as a picture of two larger fish in pursuit of smaller fry. The colors were vivid and the fish looked determined, but the souvenir allowance for Americans from Cuba was strictly for music and art.

Sally chuckled to herself, "After all, these do make a picture, so why not art!"

Afterwards Sally and Deena joined others for lunch outdoors. Lunch at the Fuster studio was served on a massive tile-encrusted table beneath an enormous mushroom canopy, also inlaid with brightly colored tiles—a glazed lagoon, quite "Alice in Wonderland." All were happy to see that the shrimp, accompanied by black beans and rice were sweet and tasted of the sea, unlike those floating throughout the tiles.

On the way back to the hotel they encountered a procession of two black Mercedes-Benz limos surrounded by a huge flock of cops on motorcycles. According to their guide, it was Fidel Castro on his way somewhere. Later that night, at dinner they could see him on a TV behind the bar, conducting one of his round table discussions to be followed by a long speech that typically would go on for hours.

On their last night in Cuba, Sally and Deena wished they

had stayed in and not joined the state sponsored dinner at the Hotel Nacional de Cuba. Dinner was fine, but the Cabaret show in the Parisian room, obligatory for all tourists was so loud that it was actually painful. Unlike the Cuban bands or the delightful flamenco show on previous evenings, this was a huge and gaudy production. Starting as a lavish history of Latin America with elaborate costumes, dancing and acrobatics; it devolved into a scantily-clad Las Vegas-type revue that would have been expected more in time of the Batista regime.

The trip back to US was almost flawless, except Deena and the other lawyers from the group were extensively questioned at the airport about where they had been and anyone they had met on the island. One guy in the group was almost detained when a Cuban official implied that he was with the CIA. Only the intervention of their official guide finally got him free.

Sally and Deena disembarked in Miami and managed to get through customs without too much hassle, though anyone returning from Cuba had their luggage searched thoroughly. The US customs official even insisted on unwrapping the small painting-sized package in Sally's carry-on bag. When the colorful tiles were revealed, Deena couldn't help but burst out laughing.

"Well, well! So, you succumbed to Señor Fustar's charming fish!" She added with a smirk, "Who is the lucky recipient?"

"A friend," Sally's smile was non-committal as she carefully rewrapped the tiles.

Silently they stepped on the escalator and headed downstairs toward the baggage claim.

Deena stepped off the escalator first and audibly gulped, "Some friend, eh?"

"That's right," came the terse reply.

"Well, that "some friend" happens to be leaning against that pillar right there."

Ilga Winicov Harrington
Falmouth, ME

Sally turned her head and grabbed Deena's arm for support as she stepped off the escalator. Brian McKinney was just straightening up from the post near the escalator, all six feet of him with a silly grin on his face. He was holding a red rose.

"Welcome home, madame!" He took a couple of steps and wrapped his arms around her in a tight hug.

Sally hugged him back and said, "I hope you still like fish."

***

Cordula Mathias
Trevett, ME

Yellows and Purple

They were just standing there
competing
for height

clustered around the power pole

the thistle with its downy flowers the
tallest,
dwarfing me by a head

followed by the finest specimen
of mullein I had ever seen

but the evening primrose was close
behind and hadn't finished
growing.

Ken Proper
Steamboat Springs, CO

We Have a Job

I have a job. Rain, shine, or pandemic, I mow the lawns. The supervisors require me to wear a mask now because I work for the city. I don't mind, during drought years it can be dusty, and then I wear one for my health. I walk to work and cut Barnum Park on Monday and Tuesday. It is a long, risky commute on public transportation during the rest of the work week to clip City Park from the zoo to the museum. I catch a streetcar at 6th Avenue, transfer at Colfax and then again at 18th. I read newspapers, novels, sometimes twice, and anything interesting. Mostly, I keep my head down, the riders are all apprehensive and in this together, but generally, the daily fear has subsided. I catch smiling eyes flashing above creative, cloth coverings.

Every day they tell me to, "Hitch up Asa," and mow the same place on the same day, which I have accomplished for years. It works for me, they let me take my stepson. The fragile boy rides the rig with me and watches the geese and birds. When necessary, the helpful child jumps off my rig, grabs the shovel and cleans up the messy piles on the lawn without being asked. The horses like him and the bosses do not make him wear a mask. Nonetheless, the creative boy imagines himself as an old west outlaw, rides shotgun and sports different colorful bandanas. "Those varmints better watch out, we have a job to do," he shouts, as I steer around sculptures of buffalo, trappers, and cowboys on wildly bucking broncos. Children require fantasies to understand the world and develop social charms. Conquering fear is lifelong endeavor. One may win the battle, but the conflict continues.

The mischievous boy needs supervision. He found a box of heavy-rail, railroad explosive signals and put a hand full on the light rails near our home. When the trolley car rolled over them, the explosion broke the windows. He got away

Ken Proper
Steamboat Springs, CO

with it, but I knew. We had a long talk about doing the right thing while the nervous adolescent clacked marbles in his pocket. I do not use the belt for punishment. He had it tough with his mother, but she disappeared one night and is gone forever, so I was told. The damaged boy believes it is his fault, but I explain we are in this together and we all have flaws. I tell him, "No man ever steps in the same river twice, for it is not the same river and he is not the same man." Norman is a good natured, quiet boy and will learn respect. I am confident he will pay attention to other folk's feelings. I say, everything in time.

I want him to go to school, but they are closed. His intricate mind has a knack for mathematics, understands abstract concepts, loves history and is handy. So, I teach him how to use tools. I tell him, "Norman, if you can't do it yourself, then you will be at the mercy of anyone with a screwdriver." We built a birdhouse and a pair of wrens moved in and raised a family. Mother and father shared the duties of the household. Both built the nest, patiently waited, and warmed the eggs. Then fetching spiders, earwigs, tasty morsels, and feeding was an adult team task. It was a joy to watch the small birds grow and hear the loud, beautiful chirps. It was cheap entertainment in tough times.

We miss the theater the most. Playbills and marques have large, rectangular, paper notices inked with "CANCELLED" pasted over descriptions of what we desire to watch. The impatient young man always wanted to arrive early and sit in the front row to hear the pianist warming her nimble fingers up, in the low light. The theater bristled with rowdiness and jazz music. Sometimes Destiny let the inquisitive child sit on the piano bench with her and she showed him C-Major scales to practice. He was curious and wanted to learn, but would rather hear the music, than practice on the silent kitchen counter. I miss her too. She was a svelte, beauty, chatty and friends with Norman's mother, Dahlia.

When the two were in a room, they created a scene of

Ken Proper
Steamboat Springs, CO

intense, wordless, power and a profound closeness like a general and a top aide. It seemed they could almost read each other's mind. When Destiny spoke, it was for the boy's benefit and mine. Last year before the pandemic, she once said directly to Norman's mother, "To grow dahlias at a mile high elevation, one must dig them up in the fall and warmly store them for the winter to plant again in the spring. If not, they freeze and die in the ground." Dahlia only nodded in agreement. She appeared to have constant apprehension like the sword of Damocles hung over her. She frequently turned on the boy with fierce, pitiless, destructive anger. He hastened to and stood behind me. When the two women spoke, it was of women's rights, choice, freedom of speech and the right to vote. Their passion worked to the inevitable conclusions and then returned to silence. They were an odd pair, one garrulous and the other reticent. Destiny talked about her life and hopes for the future. Dahlia did not.

Destiny's father owns the theater and is anxious to reopen. The streets are abandoned, and every public venue closed. Maybe, the city will let the theaters open before the pandemic ends. It is the only piano for my stepson to play. When the pubescent boy and I are alone, he asks about girls and I try to explain their capricious feminine desires. "Listen to what females say and remember everything comes in time." The tall, awkward boy's eyes reveal the mystery continues.

He wants a dog and I say a puppy on the rig would be difficult. I will give in eventually; the lonely boy needs another companion. Learning responsibility by feeding, caring, training, and cleaning up will teach him to be a compassionate adult. He already is quite handy with a shovel and we have a large, fenced yard.

We spend every evening in the garden behind the house. The vegetables are heavy with produce and the dahlia flowers bloom with a spectacular array of colors. The helpful boy weeds with me and once asked, "Is Mother dead in the

Ken Proper
Steamboat Springs, CO

ground?"

My answer, "I believe so, son." He was uneasy and started to hum a tune. Then we sang, "The worms crawl in, the worms crawl out, and they play pinochle in your snout. When you die and turn all green, then you become a viral machine."

I will continue to teach him to do the right thing, encourage his education and train him to be a kind, thoughtful man. I will try to be a good father to a frightened boy who started as a stranger and needed a friend. The intriguing teenager will help me weed the garden in the evening, sing silly songs and dig up the dahlias in the fall.

I enjoy his company and watching him mature. He has a potentially bright future and dreams are his to grasp. Maybe he will play the piano and fall in love with a dog or someone special. Time will tell.

Heraclitus, the ancient Greek philosopher wrote, "It is disease that makes health sweet." The darn pandemic virus has made us closer, but I hope in 1919 he can go back to school, and we can ride the trolley to the theater. The valuable boy can pick up the piles of horse manure behind the mower in the summer and when the dog arrives, all year round.

It is said, "There is nothing permanent except change." Sadly, the little, baby, birds grew up and flew the coop. Youngsters grow up quickly and then they leave.

Lucia Owen
Stoneham, ME

What I Saw

How casual to cartoon him goofy,
part horse, part cow, part camel,
improbable assembly of spare parts

Until the evening he gave shape
to the twilight
and walked the dirt road
along the lake shore.

His steps, the forward flick of his ears
the only motion,
his breath
the only sound.

He turned down to the water
his hocks a glint of white.
The only sound then
the faint slap-slap
as he lipped.

He stood, turned,
then shifted a shoulder
in between some saplings
and vanished in the dark.
The trees did not move

Or notice me.

Darrell McBreairty
Allagash, ME

Witness

Like shadows slipping
beneath the setting sun
they disappear
leaving me as lone witness
to the history of the implements
employed by generations
of our family
and I stand alone at the edge
of the stone yard
listening to their voices
as they grow fainter
with the passing years.

The rolling pins and hammers
and teacups I cannot couple
with the names of those
who once possessed them
will become just ordinary pieces
stacked in yard sales
and scattered into the black hole
of oblivion
that swallows up
that which is not named.

Debbie Broderick
Limerick, ME

The Interminable Search

Trina woke with a jolt. Her unsettling dream had jump-started her day in high alert mode, infusing her with a sense of unease. She knew that her waking hours would now be colored by that persistently disturbed feeling that lingered after waking in the middle of a distressing dream. She was annoyed, since it was the first day of her spring vacation as a Kindergarten teacher, and she'd been looking forward to a calm and relaxing week at home away from stress and kids.

In her dream, she'd been searching endlessly for her ex-boyfriend's name in the phone book, but had not been able to locate it. In real life, she'd have known his number, obviously, but this was her subconscious at work. There was nothing logical about the dream scenario, of her desperately needing to make a call to him. It was somehow critical that she reach him, a kind of life or death situation. She knew how to spell his last name. She just couldn't **find** it. She'd kept trying, but her search was futile—his last name, a common one, seemed to have vanished from the pages. Just as she got to the section that should have had his name next, there were pages and pages of advertisements before the next listing. She flicked past them to resume looking through the list, but the names that appeared next were alphabetically beyond what she was looking for. She flipped backwards again, thinking she might have missed it, but no, it definitely wasn't there. She felt panicky, a sense of dread and terror seeping through her as she kept repeating the same actions over and over again, with the same alarming outcome—no resolution! The more frantic she became, the more chaotic her efforts were.

But now that she was awake, that constant feeling of being in limbo, of not having had a conclusive outcome to her puzzling dream sequence, left Trina feeling unnerved. It had been years since she'd had to use a phone book, so she was

Debbie Broderick
Limerick, ME

perplexed about that outdated look-up being the source of her frustration. Yes, she still insisted that a novel was best read on paper, but she certainly didn't feel the same way about data searches. And so a feeling of unease, of having an unresolved, nagging issue hanging over her, permeated her thoughts while she cooked her morning oatmeal. Her thoughts distracted her from monitoring the porridge, and it overflowed in the microwave. "Noooooooooo.....!" she hissed. Now she had a horrible, pasty mess to deal with.

She gazed through the raindrop-studded window as she ate what was left of her breakfast, feeling glad that the dreary, grey rain had stopped falling, at least. It was still pretty windy, and the anemic sunshine, though too ineffectual to produce shadows on the ground, hinted that it might be possible to dry her laundry outdoors today. She'd always loved both the fresh aroma and the crispness of line-dried clothing, perhaps because it was a nostalgic reminder of home, but her schedule at school precluded doing this on a regular basis. It was a small luxury she decided to indulge herself in now that she had some time at home. Perhaps it would also help improve her mood, she thought, so she resolutely began that chore right after the breakfast clean up.

She rummaged about in her messy, disordered under-the-sink collection of detergents, unable to find the stain remover. She found herself doing the same as she'd done in her dream—looking through the same items over and over, repetitively, assuming she was looking in the right place, and it might suddenly appear. *Dang, she'd have to do her laundry without it today,* she'd concluded, disgruntled. As she stood up, she spied the delinquent bottle standing behind the faucet, where she'd left it after trying to get mud-season splash off her dress pants. Thus far, it seemed as if everything about her day was unsatisfactory. She had an overwhelming sense that, no matter what she tried, and no matter how hard she tried, nothing would work out today. It seemed that everything would inevitably go wrong; that the

Debbie Broderick
Limerick, ME

moody cloud ominously suspended over her thoughts was certain to ruin anything and everything she attempted that day.

The only thing for it, she thought, after hanging her laundry in the gusty spring wind, *was to take a walk outdoors.* That should loosen the wintery mood-webs clogging her mind. It was either that, or curl up under her bedclothes and spend the day perseverating over her dream. She thought the walk would help her sort through her thoughts, perhaps even shake off the relentless searching sensation, and allow her to salvage the rest of her day. She was determined to free herself of that feeling of being trapped in an endless loop. The spiraling search icon that came up on her computer screen whenever she shopped for books online, was the best representation of her mind right now.

Setting off on her cleansing walk, she saw the rags of winter strewn about everywhere she looked—untidy snow remnants were caught amidst the dense tangle of blackberry brambles, and in sheltered ditches that had been in shadow longer than others. The roadside edges were a dirty mess of grit-coated snow clumps. The wind gusts had increased noticeably, and she wondered how safe her single-wide was in the woods, as she watched the boughs at the top of the canopy twisting and twirling, as if they might shear off. Trina cringed as she imagined the sensation of their rough, licheny limbs scraping against each other, rasping like coarse sandpaper. She branched off the road and made her way alongside the pond abutting her development, noticing three large blobs floating near the edges of the dark water. At first glance, she thought they might be dislodged ice chunks bobbing, or possibly discarded plastic bags, but as she got closer, she recognized, what was for her, an irrefutable harbinger of spring: the glaringly white, low riding Common Mergansers, en route to their summer homes! She was glad she'd got outside today to witness this most welcome sight, an uplifting sign of the season's forward progress.

Debbie Broderick
Limerick, ME

She was almost home when she became aware of faint, eerie sounds. She stopped frequently to check what it could be—the tall, flexible boughs were intermittently catching on each other still—sighing, groaning, and creaking—but what she'd tuned in to was an indistinct sound, like a light whistle. She realized slowly, like a cloud shadow spreading over a landscape, that it was her own breathing that she was hearing! *Oh heck, my asthma...*she realized, rather sheepishly, automatically patting the pockets of her windbreaker for that hard, familiar canister that would help ease her wheezing. Failing to feel anything remotely solid in her jacket pockets, she felt panic rise, as she continued the same frantic motions over and over again—relentless, repetitive, fruitless searching! She couldn't seem to stop herself from rummaging about, hoping that her back and forth efforts would eventually produce the result she sought. *Figure this out,* she admonished herself, as she vainly reached into the internal pockets, when her inhaler was clearly not there either.

All she could do now, was go directly home in as steady and calm a manner as possible, to get to her medication. As she drew alongside her little yard, she found herself admiring the perfect color gradation of the laundry she'd hung earlier—today's palette ranged seamlessly from an array of greens to various blues, through to purples, and all the way to black. *Geez, way to display my idiosyncratic tendencies to the whole world,* she mused to herself. *But it truly is a perfect color sequence at the same time,* she thought proudly.

Back inside, she found her inhaler of course, lying on the window sill next to her front door. After dosing herself with a couple of quick puffs, she felt comfortable that she was responding appropriately to the albuterol, as she usually did. She made herself a cup of Chai, warming some rich, light cream in her microwave, and adding a small cinnamon stick for that extra zingy flavor she loved. She cradled the hot mug in her palms to warm her hands, and settled onto the couch with the intent of reading her book. It was a memoir by a

Maine author, checking two of her boxes of preferred reading material.

As the spiced, warm tea seeped through her, it dawned on Trina that there had been a series of searches throughout her day thus far, both in her dream and in real life. *I guess that's what my life is all about right now,* she thought miserably, *an endless search.* Though she'd tried to recoup her day, she was still struck by that insistent sense of creeping unease. It felt similar to getting to the end of a book or movie with a totally unfulfilling ending, that left one disturbed and longing for answers.

At the sound of unanticipated activity at her front door, she relinquished her self-indulgent musings and went to investigate. There was a delivery guy standing there holding a large package, which she realized would be her latest book order. She was thrilled with this knowledge, believing it to be a definite positive in her otherwise lack-luster day. She opened the door and took the box from him, becoming instantaneously aware of the heftiness of the package, his handling of which had belied its weight.

"Aah, fantastic! My books! My books!" she shrieked delightedly, wondering to herself whether he'd noticed her inadvertently crumpling with the initial weight of it, as he let go. She hoped her expressive excitement had camouflaged her weakness.

"Books? You mean real books? I don't often come across people our age, who read actual, physical books," he offered. "There are so few of us left! I'm really happy to meet a fellow bibliophile," he added, good-naturedly.

"Yeah, it's cool to know that there are other people who appreciate the real thing, too. I love being able to touch and turn the pages, you know? To feel the paper between my fingertips, and sense the unfolding of the story," Trina shared, having lowered the book carton onto the trunk in her mudroom.

"Me too!" he assured her, appreciatively. He seemed to

Debbie Broderick
Limerick, ME

hesitate just then, unsure of what to say next, then turned to leave. After a few steps towards his truck, he swung back towards her, his face aglow. "Also, um, I saw that you hang your laundry outside, and it's...well...it's...um...I hope you don't mind me saying this, but...well, I'm totally impressed with your color gradation on the wash-line. It's freakin' awesome. How'd you do that?"

Trina felt a slow warmth spread inside her. Was it her hot tea bringing on this flush? There was something so affirming about what he'd said. It was comforting and...well, it made her feel...a connection. And it felt nice. Was this a turn-around to her day? To her life? Could this mean her search was over, she wondered? Was her looping, searching quest over at last?

After quickly checking that her phone number was on the shipping label, she tore it off the package and handed it to him, boldly saying, "Here's my number. I'd love to explain my laundry palette to you after your shift. I'm Trina. Give me a call."

"Seriously? This must be my lucky day. I'll give you a call later...Trina!" he grinned, then walked away, pumping his hand into the air. He spun around again and added, "Oh, and I'm Danny, by the way."

***

Sally Belenardo
Branford, CT

Airport Food

At JFK, a
vulture sat on an airplane
with his carrion.

Judy Driscoll Winchenbaugh
Rockland, ME

The Apple Tree

Every day since the accident, I've had to drive past that tree. The one the three of us, my family, used to drive by. But now I'm the only one left. Somedays I wonder why I'm still here. Miss them both so much. My husband. Our son. Ten years, the best of my life, gone. Just like that. Just because the other driver was texting and didn't see the stop sign.

It's not just that apple tree. It's every apple tree. Whenever I see one, the anger, the survivor's guilt, the grief all hit me like a tsunami. Sometimes I have to stop myself from turning that wheel, stepping on the gas and driving into the scarred trunk. Then I wouldn't be alone anymore. But at the last minute I stop myself. Don't know why.

It happened at the end of our street. The other driver didn't see the stop sign. Hit our Taurus, pushing it headfirst into the old apple tree on the corner. That tree was the last one from the old orchard dug up when the houses were built here. We used to watch the seasons change with the apple tree. Spring with the beautiful fragrant blossoms, summer watching the fruit grow, fall we joined the other families picking the fresh, ripe apples. The neighborhood kids had so much fun collecting apples, the brave ones climbing high branches to reach the best ones. Then in winter we watched the bare branches survive against the ice and snow. Now I can't bear to see that tree. The scar on the trunk where the car hit. Every time my world falls apart, again. Maybe someday the bark will grow back on the trunk, but the scar on my heart will never heal.

Debbie, my best friend, is my rock. While I was working my two weeks' notice at the bank, she packed up the memories and sorted them for me. Boxes for my new place. Boxes to donate. Then the rest. What I couldn't, just couldn't, deal with. Too difficult. Too hard. Too sad. Debbie understood

Judy Driscoll Winchenbaugh
Rockland, ME

without asking. She rented a storage unit in my new town and stored those boxes. Told me when I'm ready, I can decide what to do with them and she'll pay the rental fees for however long it takes.

God Bless Debbie. She was the first one I called when the sheriff came to the door that day. I blabbered and cried so, Debbie rushed over, concerned when she couldn't understand what I was trying to say. The sheriff talked to her, told her the details. I was in shock, disbelief. Still am, even after all these months.

Today is my last day at the house. Debbie is here with me. We walk through each room, the memories bouncing off the walls in waves. The Christmas tree with Timmy's homemade decorations. The window seat Ken and I cuddled on at night, watching the stars. I touch the built-in hutch in the dining room Ken built. I take a picture of the wall where we marked Timmy's height each year on his birthday. Ten marks. I try to blink back the tears, but a few escape.

A fresh start. That's what everyone told me. It would do me good. Start over, build a new life with new memories. As though the old life could be forgotten. As though the last ten years of marriage and family never happened. So I listened. Put the house up for sale, our dream home. But, oh, the memories that are in that home. Some bring smiles, some bring tears, but all those memories tear at my heart.

The house is sold. A new family will make memories. The master bedroom will have someone else's furniture, the other bedroom might be painted pink instead of blue. I bought a condo in the city, found a new job at another bank. No parks with trees near my new home. An adults only complex. All new furniture, memories packed away in that storage unit. I know, deep in my heart, they would want me to carry on. So, for them, I will try.

It's time to leave. I lock the door for the last time, give the key to Debbie for the realtor. Outside, we hug, wipe at our tears. Debbie hands me a silver necklace, a heart engraved

Judy Driscoll Winchenbaugh
Rockland, ME

with Ken and Timmy's initials. I stand next to the rose bush Ken gave me on our last anniversary, watching Debbie cut through the neighbor's lawn, back to her house. Her family.

Then I back out of that driveway. Drive to the end of the street. That apple tree is still there, defiant. My wheel turns, my foot on the gas pedal.

***

Robert B. Moreland
Pleasant Prairie, WI

Rite of Spring

Gravel prairie road,
doe pauses in bright headlights
leaping half-filled ditch.

April's first fawn in her belly
jolts her flight, kicks with new life.

Moreland, R.B. (2013) 2014 Wisconsin Poets Calendar *"Rite of Spring"* page 32.

Robert B. Moreland
Pleasant Prairie, WI

West Feliciana Parish Blues

To the southwest, lightning illuminates
cloudbanks lurking in the humid spring night.
Mississippi artery pumps russet flows
in silence as the old New Roads Ferry
makes its last run across roiling currents.
It has been storming all day this Easter,
tepid clouds stirred early, blocking the sun
while by hot mid-afternoon, thunder growled.
Four generations of family gathered,
tornado watches announced across the
parish as egg hunts and tosses occurred
beneath tumultuous, threatening skies.
Heavens opened, rain's staccato drumbeat
on the tin roof reached a fever pitched roar.
The Louisiana lilt of words piqued
my ear; Southern born, my tongue "yankee-fied"
by years spent in Boston and the Midwest.
The simple beauty of life's brief waltz was
captured in congregations of babies
and growing children of children; seeing
the mortal in the immortality
of it all. How fleeting is this life! We
live as though we feign forever yet have
but a mayfly's day. As the hourglass
drips sand and the numbered heartbeats reach their
end, the aging partners postpone their dance
surprised when the clock begins to chime midnight.

Moreland, R.B. (2014) "West Feliciana Blues" *The Penwood Review* 18(1): 13.